# THE MYSTERY of the THIRD LUCRETIA

# THE
# MYSTERY
## *of the* THIRD
# LUCRETIA

*Susan Runholt*

VIKING

VIKING

Published by Penguin Group

Penguin Young Readers Group, 345 Hudson Street, New York, New York 10014, U.S.A.

Penguin Group (Canada), 90 Eglinton Avenue East, Suite 700, Toronto, Ontario, Canada
M4P 2Y3 (a division of Pearson Penguin Canada Inc.)

Penguin Books Ltd, 80 Strand, London WC2R 0RL, England

Penguin Ireland, 25 St Stephen's Green, Dublin 2, Ireland (a division of Penguin Books Ltd)

Penguin Group (Australia), 250 Camberwell Road, Camberwell, Victoria 3124, Australia
(a division of Pearson Australia Group Pty Ltd)

Penguin Books India Pvt Ltd, 11 Community Centre, Panchsheel Park, New Delhi – 110 017, India

Penguin Group (NZ), 67 Apollo Drive, Rosedale, North Shore 0632, New Zealand
(a division of Pearson New Zealand Ltd.)

Penguin Books (South Africa) (Pty) Ltd, 24 Sturdee Avenue, Rosebank, Johannesburg 2196, South Africa

Penguin Books Ltd, Registered Offices: 80 Strand, London WC2R 0RL, England

First published in 2008 by Viking, a division of Penguin Young Readers Group

10  9  8  7  6  5  4  3  2  1

LIBRARY OF CONGRESS CATALOGING-IN-PUBLICATION DATA

Runholt, Susan.
The mystery of the third Lucretia / by Susan Runholt.
p. cm.
Summary: While traveling in London, Paris, and Amsterdam, fourteen-year-old best friends
Kari and Lucas solve an international art forgery mystery.
ISBN 978-0-670-06252-2 (hardcover)
[1. Mystery and detective stories. 2. Art—Forgeries—Fiction. 3. Best friends—Fiction.
4. Friendship—Fiction. 5. Travel—Fiction. 6. Europe—Fiction.] I. Title.
PZ7.R888293My 2008
[Fic]—dc22
2007024009

Printed in USA
Set in CG Cloister
Book design by Jim Hoover

For my mother, Helen,
who always believed in me,
and my daughter, Annalisa, who
helped me write this book.

# Beginnings

My name is Kari Sundgren. This story is about how my best friend Lucas and I got mixed up in a big international art crime, and all the adventures we had doing it. Lucas is Lucas Stickney. She's a girl.

My ninth-grade English book says when you're telling a complicated story, unless you're a real expert, it's usually best to begin at the beginning and go all the way to the end. That makes sense.

But since I read that, I've noticed that finding the beginning of a story, especially when your story is a complicated one, isn't always as easy as it sounds. Some stories don't seem to have a beginning. They just sort of happen because of a lot of things that have been going on for a long time. And some stories have too many beginnings. You could start almost anywhere.

This story is like that. It has a lot of beginnings. I

could start it when we noticed the guy painting at the Art Institute, or when we saw him again in London, or in Paris when we saw the article in the *Herald Tribune*, or in the museum in Amsterdam—well, you get the idea. So I asked my English teacher how you find the real beginning of a story, and he said it's the first thing that happened that you have to explain.

That's what I was afraid he was going to say.

So I guess I have to start twenty-six centuries ago. In Rome.

Lucretia was this woman who supposedly lived in the sixth century BCE. This was, like, when they used to have gladiators. She was married to a Roman soldier who was always bragging about what a wonderful, good, pure, loving woman his wife was.

When he was off fighting some war, a guy named Sextus Tarquinius, one of his rivals, sneaked back to Rome and flirted with Lucretia to try to get her to have an affair with him. She wouldn't, so he raped her.

Now back in those days it wasn't bad enough that a woman had that kind of thing happen to her. What made it even worse was that it totally wrecked her reputation. A lot of women who got attacked like that would have been kicked out of their house. It was the kind of thing that makes my mother go on and on about what a rotten deal women have always gotten. I have to admit, it does seem pretty unfair.

Anyway, Lucretia was a truly good person. So she

called her husband and her father back from the war and told them about what had happened to her. They said it wasn't her fault and it wasn't that big of a deal. But because it was so dishonorable, she picked up a dagger and killed herself. Can you believe that? Even though she didn't do anything wrong!

By the way, I'm not making this up. This may not be absolutely true, but it's a real legend. Google it.

The second part of the story happened in Amsterdam way back in the 1600s. You probably know this, but Amsterdam is a city in the Netherlands, which is in Europe. It's the place where they have windmills, and where people used to wear wooden shoes. Anyway, there was this painter named Rembrandt van Rijn. Nowadays most people just call him Rembrandt. You've maybe heard of him, and you might even have seen some of his paintings if you go to museums. He even has a toothpaste named after him.

Rembrandt painted two pictures of Lucretia. In one, she's all dressed up in a beautiful white and gold gown, and she's holding a dagger like she's getting ready to stab herself. In the other picture she's already stabbed herself, her dress is hanging loose, and there's blood coming out of her side. Lucretia's expression in the paintings is so sad. It just makes you feel sorry for her.

Now, you probably know this, but if you don't I'll tell you, because it's going to be important. Old paintings by famous artists are worth a lot of money. Millions. Sometimes millions and millions. So far the artist whose painting has sold for the most money is a guy named Gustav Klimt, who painted pictures that have lots of little gold squares and twirls and things in the background. Anyway, one of his paintings sold for $135 million, if you can believe that.

But Rembrandt's pictures are also worth a lot. As artists go, he's a Very Big Deal. Let's say somebody found a painting by Rembrandt that nobody had discovered before. They could probably sell it for twenty or thirty million dollars. Maybe more, depending on how beautiful and interesting it was.

I'm telling you this because it's what makes everything else in the story make sense. The man in the galleries, the picture of the dead Lucretia, the car that almost ran over Lucas, the kidnapping—none of that would have happened if old paintings weren't worth a humongous amount of money.

# Lucas the Lionheart

Lucas and I met four years ago, when we were both ten. We were taking a summer drawing course at a museum called the Minneapolis Institute of Arts, which everyone calls the Art Institute.

I hated her right away.

There were eight of us in the class, all from different schools, so I didn't know anybody. Lucas and I had easels side by side, but we didn't start talking until it was almost lunch break. All morning we'd been working on drawing a basket with a bunch of fruit in it and some cherries scattered around the side. We were all kind of circled around this table with the fruit on it, so none of us could see anybody else's drawing. The teacher walked around and muttered privately to every student.

When he was muttering to somebody on the other side

of the room, Lucas turned to me and whispered, "This your first class?"

I said, "Yeah. This *your* first class?"

She shook her head. "I've been taking classes for three years."

I didn't say anything else for a while, so finally she said, "Can I see your drawing?"

"Sure," I said, "if I can see yours." I was proud of what I'd done. I always felt like I was pretty good in art. My dad is a professional artist, and he helped me learn how to draw and paint. All my life I'd gotten As in art. Even that morning the teacher had looked at my picture a few times and told me I was doing a good job. I was secretly hoping I'd be the best one in the class.

So Lucas came over to my easel and said, "That's really good." And of course I was proud.

Then we went over to look at Lucas's picture. I couldn't believe it. She'd drawn the basket and the fruit perfectly. *Perfectly.* And she'd put in shading, and even drawn the pattern in the tablecloth. It looked like something somebody would put a frame on and hang over their fireplace.

It really ticked me off. I figured she just said my picture was good because she felt sorry for me. Okay, I admit it. I was also jealous because she was better than I was.

It turned out she was better than anybody. She was the best in the whole class, easy. I think even the teacher was impressed. After that first morning I didn't talk to Lucas the whole rest of the week.

About a month later I was standing in line to get a cone at an ice-cream place near my house. Somebody behind me said, "Kari?" and I turned around, and there was Lucas.

It was a surprise. Neither of us knew the other one lived in Saint Paul. She went—well, I guess I should say she goes—to this really fancy private school, and I go to a regular public school.

By the way, for those of you who are bad in geography, maybe I'd better explain that Minneapolis and Saint Paul are right across the Mississippi River from each other. That's why they call them the Twin Cities. It's all like one big town, and people go back and forth all the time, so it's not a surprise that our class was at a museum in Minneapolis, even though we're from Saint Paul.

Anyway, we might not have gotten to be friends even then if it hadn't been for the idiot clerk in the ice-cream shop. Here Lucas and I were, next in line, ready to buy ice-cream cones, and the girl just ignored us. Yeah, we were only ten. But that wasn't any reason she should wait on everybody else before us.

But she did. First there were two women who ordered complicated sundaes. When they were finished, the two of us looked up, ready to give our orders. But the clerk looked right over our heads and took an order from a man and his two little kids.

"This stinks!" Lucas said.

"It's totally not fair," I said. I was whispering, but it was a loud whisper.

Now, you probably can't tell it from how I treated Lucas in that class, but I can be kind of timid. Lately I've been getting better, but when I was ten I was really shy. I don't suppose I'd have said anything to the ice-cream clerk even if I'd been waiting for an hour.

But Lucas isn't timid *at all*. She wants to be an environmental lawyer when she grows up, and I feel sorry for the lumber and oil companies she goes out to get. You'd never know it to look at her—she's thin, has curly reddish blond hair and glasses, kind of cute, and looks like any normal kid—but inside she's tough. I call her Lucas the Lionheart.

So when the clerk took the money from the man and began looking over our heads at the adults around us to find her next customer, Lucas banged her fist down on the counter and said, "We were here before your last two sets of customers, and if you don't serve us next, I'm going to report you to your manager."

Remember, Lucas was ten.

Everybody in the store looked at us, and I thought I was going to die of embarrassment. But we got our ice-cream cones, and when we got outside we started laughing and we've been friends ever since.

We took another museum course together that summer, this time in painting, and I found out I'm better at that than she is. She draws well because she can remember almost every single thing she's ever seen in her life and draw it the way it looked. Her mind works like that. They call it photographic memory. Also, she's very careful and tries to get everything exactly right. I think the word is *analytical*. I don't have photographic memory and I'm not very analytical, but I'm more creative than she is. I'm good with color and composition, and I can come up with new ideas.

She draws what she sees perfectly. I see something and make something new out of it. We make a good team.

# 3

# Gallery Guy

Okay, here's another beginning. The first time we saw Gallery Guy.

Now, most of this story happened last spring and summer in London and Amsterdam and a little bit in Paris. But this part happened right here in Minnesota more than a year before that, before I turned thirteen.

One of Rembrandt's two *Lucretia*s is owned by the Minneapolis Institute of Arts, the place where Lucas and I took the classes. It's the second one, where she's already stabbed herself and her dress is bloody. Mom and I have been going to the Art Institute for as long as I can remember. We were able to go even when we were poor, because it's free.

I like lots of things in the museum, but for some reason I've always been totally interested in the *Lucretia* painting. It's not that she's so beautiful or anything, because she's not, really. It's more because of her story and because she looks so sad. And also because I just like the way Rembrandt paints.

Anyway, the Art Institute was having an exhibit where they showed both of Rembrandt's *Lucretia* paintings. The second of the *Lucretia*s is owned by the National Gallery in Washington, D.C. The two museums got together and shared them that year for a special exhibit. So for a while both paintings were in Washington, then they were here. Or maybe it was the other way around. Whatever. Anyway, Mom and Lucas and I made a special trip to see the paintings one night.

I don't know if you've ever spent much time in a museum, but if you have you've probably seen somebody with an easel set up, copying a painting. This happens in almost every museum. In fact, when Lucas and I were taking those art classes at the Art Institute, we had to go out and copy from the paintings in the galleries. My mom says that people who aren't taking a museum's art classes have to apply and get special permission in advance. Mostly they're art students from colleges, but almost anyone can get permission to copy a painting if they just ask.

Well, that night there was this guy copying one of the *Lucretia*s. He had kind of thick, mostly gray hair in a ponytail. Mom and Lucas weren't especially interested in what he was doing, but I was. Maybe it was because I'd spent so much time watching my dad paint. Anyway, this guy had his stool in one corner and his easel was turned so you couldn't see what he was painting unless you walked around it on purpose.

I wanted to see how it looked when somebody copied a painting, but first I wanted to learn all about the two paintings in the exhibit. There were a lot of big signs on the walls telling about Rembrandt, and about Lucretia and ancient Rome, and I wanted to read everything. Lucas stayed with me in the little exhibit room while Mom looked at the paintings in the main gallery just outside. There weren't many visitors in the museum that night, so Lucas and I were alone in the *Lucretia* room except for the man at the easel.

Finally I finished looking at the pictures and reading about them, and I wanted to go over and look at what the guy was painting. So I walked over to the corner where he was sitting and started to kind of slink around behind his easel.

I was just ready to ask him if I could look at his painting when he said, "Go a-*way*." In fact, he didn't say it so much as he snarled it. "Go a-*way*." Just like that. I wasn't sure, but it sounded like he might have an accent.

I turned around and started walking out of the gallery really fast. Lucas was coming the other way, toward the guy, as if she was going to ream him out for being mean to me or something, but I caught her arm and said, "Let's just get out of here," and she came along.

From that day on we started calling the man Gallery Guy. It was a bad enough experience that it kind of stuck in my mind. And although it wasn't very much fun when it happened, it's a good thing he told me to go a-*way*, or we would never have solved the mystery of the *Third Lucretia*.

# My Parents, a Magazine, Traveling, and Me

Okay, you've met Lucas, Lucretia, Rembrandt, and Gallery Guy. It's probably time you got to know a little bit about the other important people in this story: my mom and me.

I was born at a very early age in Saint Paul, Minnesota. My parents have been divorced since I was three. My father is Karl Sundgren. Like I said, he's a painter. Which is probably why I like to draw and paint. A genetic thing. He lives on a houseboat in a little town on the Mississippi River. I usually go stay with him a few weekends during the school year and for a week during the summer.

He's great on the weekends. But the time I spend with him in the summer isn't as much fun. It always starts out fine—we go fishing and he teaches me to paint—but after about a week I'm glad to go home to my mom in Saint Paul. It's not that I don't love him, but I start to feel in the way.

I think it's because he likes to party and have girlfriends around, and he can't really do those things when I'm there. Besides, it's a *small* houseboat, and it gets crowded.

Mom is Gillian Welles Sundgren. Her first name is pronounced like *Jillian*, but it's spelled the English way. She's kind of tall, has green eyes and naturally curly black hair. I look like Mom, only I'm shorter, my hair isn't as curly, and my eyes are more hazel than green.

Mom works for *The Scene* magazine. If you get *The Scene*, look in the front where everyone who works on it is listed. That's called the masthead. Usually they make you look through about a million pages of advertising before you find it. Now, see where it says "Contributing Editors"? She's the fourth one down.

It says "International—Europe" next to her name because she does a lot of stories from outside the United States. I have to admit, it's pretty cool having a mother who writes international stories for one of America's most popular magazines for teenagers. But believe me, it wasn't always like this.

For a long time Mom had a job writing for a newspaper. She didn't make much money, but eventually she saved up enough to take me to England for two weeks. When we got back, she wrote some articles about it during her spare time, sent them to *The Scene*, and they liked what she wrote and offered her this job. They said she'd need to be out of the country about three months during the year.

She thought about it for a long time. She wanted the job. The problem was me.

We talked about it one night when we were both getting ready for bed. The discussion started while we were brushing our teeth. Then we moved to my room.

"Why can't I just stay with Dad while you're gone, at least during the summer and school holidays?" I asked as I pulled on the "Greetings from Ancient Troy" T-shirt I wear to bed.

"Forget about it," Mom said. She was sitting cross-legged on the foot of my bed. "You have trouble staying with him for a week. How could you stand it for a month at a time?"

"Well, how about Uncle Geoff? I don't get tired of him, and he lives right downstairs."

"He has a busy life. We can't expect him to give it up to stay home with you if I'm gone for more than a week. Besides, he's out on a dig half the time."

Uncle Geoffrey, Mom's brother, teaches archeology at the university and goes to Turkey and Greece and Egypt three or four times during the school year and all summer to dig up ruins. He's the one who brought me my Ancient Troy T-shirt.

"Well, how about if you took me along and scheduled your trips for the summer and during school vacations? I want to go back to Europe. Can't I, please?" I was sitting up in bed by that time, and now I was trying to wear my most angelic look. Sometimes that works.

"I'd love to take you, honey. You don't know how much." Mom looked like she wanted to fling her arms around me. Fortunately she was sitting too far away. "But I have to work, and you'd be locked up in our hotel rooms like a prisoner. Plus you'd miss a lot of school.

"And don't say," she said, holding up her hand like a traffic cop, "that I should get somebody to go with us. I've already thought about hiring a tutor, but I can't afford it."

So that was the end of that discussion. But she kept thinking about it. And I kept thinking about it. And then I told Lucas, and she figured out what to do.

5

# From Allen the Meep to the Gleesome Threesome

I've learned a lot from Lucas since we got to know each other, and the first thing I learned was that money doesn't buy happiness.

When I met Lucas, I was used to not being rich and I never minded it that much. Mom and I always had a good time even when we were broke. We found lots of things to do for free or cheap and we never were hungry or homeless or anything, which is luckier than a lot of people. But I guess somehow I thought rich people were automatically happier than poor people.

Wrong.

Lucas's family has tons of cash, and they're miserable.

Lucas's dad is a very big-deal lawyer here in the Twin Cities. He's been the lawyer for some really famous cases. Do you remember when that petroleum plant blew up in

Saudi Arabia and all those American employees were killed and injured? Well, Allen Stickney was the lawyer who sued the company, Ibis Petroleum, and got over a billion dollars for his clients. He was on the network news and CNN and *The NewsHour* on PBS.

Lucas has a nickname for her father, Allen the A——. It's a word I can't say, and I'll probably get in trouble for even putting in this much. Lucas and I came up with a word we substitute for words like that. Our word is *meep*. Like, we say, "That meeping teacher," or "Oh, meep, I forgot my library book again." So when we're around people, we call Lucas's dad Allen the Meep.

There are so many things wrong with Allen the Meep that it's hard to know where to start. The thing that makes me maddest is that he's rotten to Lucas. He never wanted to have a girl, because he's a chauvinist pig through and through, so half the time he ignores Lucas and the other half he yells at her. I've never seen him hug her. Not even once. Lucas doesn't talk about it much. Still, I know it bothers her a lot that her dad doesn't seem to love her, or even like her a whole lot.

It's more peaceful when Mr. Stickney is off on a case, which he is most of the time, but Mrs. Stickney is no prize, either. Her name is Camellia. She's from the South. She has gorgeous red hair, full lips, big blue eyes, perfect skin, big boobs, and long legs. She's absolutely, unbelievably gorgeous. But that's about it. She's just this sort of beautiful, empty person. She's not stupid. Not at all. But all she thinks about are her looks and her clothes and getting away from her husband's temper tantrums by flying off to see her fancy friends in Santa Fe and La Jolla and the Bahamas.

Until last year, when Lucas turned thirteen and her brother went away to school, they always had a nanny because the Fair Camellia, as Lucas calls her, can't be bothered spending too much time taking care of her own kids.

I know I'm making her sound like a monster, and she isn't, really. I think she loves her children, and I think she feels bad that her husband isn't nicer to Lucas. It's just that she's so interested in herself and clothes and other things that have to do with money that sometimes her kids don't seem very important to her.

Then there's Justin, who's eleven now and thinks he's God's gift to the human race. But he's actually one of the world's most obnoxious creatures. We call him the Brat Child. In fact he was such a problem in his school that the Stickneys had to send him off to a private academy. Believe it or not, he's the only person Mr. Stickney isn't mean to. He says Justin is just high-spirited.

High-spirited my meep. The kid's a menace.

Lucas would probably be a little messed up with all these weird people around her if it weren't for her grandmother. Mom says Lucas's grandma Stickney is one of the world's great human beings. She's really been important to Lucas. She's smart and loving and interesting, and Lucas is just like her. Lucas even looks like pictures of her grandmother when she was young. Grandma Stickney was the one who taught Lucas to be interested in the environment and women's rights, and to think that who she is inside is more important than the way she looks. Obviously Allen the Meep, her son, takes after his father, who's been dead for years.

When Lucas was younger she used to stay with her grandma a lot. But for the past few years, Grandma Stickney's been the head of an international organization that's trying to improve the way women are treated around the world, so now she's out of town most of the time going to conferences and making speeches.

So that's Lucas's family.

I remember one of the first times I'd been over at their house on a Saturday. Camellia and Allen the Meep were yelling at each other, the Brat Child had his TV blasting in the bedroom next to Lucas's, and when Lucas asked him to turn it down he swore at her at the top of his lungs. Later we went to the kitchen to have some ice cream and get away from Justin's blaring TV, and there was a note from Camellia saying she'd gone out shopping and wouldn't even be back for dinner.

Just about that time my cell phone rang and it was Mom. "Hi, sweetie!" she said. "I've got an idea. I was thinking we should live it up a little tonight, so I got us some movies at the library and I thought we'd order a pizza. Do you want to ask Lucas to stay overnight?"

I was totally glad to hear her voice. It sounded so normal, and so did the part about the pizza and DVDs. Up until then I'd been a little embarrassed to have Lucas come over to my house. See, she lives in a mansion on an exclusive street and we live in an upstairs duplex, and at that time we didn't have really nice furniture or anything.

But the things that had happened that afternoon were enough to teach me that I was a lot luckier than Lucas, money or no money.

So I asked her, and she came over and stayed the whole next day until it was time to go to bed on Sunday night. Since then I think she's spent more time at my house than she has at hers.

She and my mom totally hit it off. So when Lucas and I were younger, the three of us pretty much did everything together. We used to call ourselves the Gleesome Threesome, back when it was fun having a parent around. We'd be in the car on our way to a camping trip and somebody would say, "The Gleesome Threesome Goes Camping." Or it would be, "The Gleesome Threesome Goes to the Zoo." We don't do it so much anymore now that Lucas and I are older and would rather not have adults around most of the time.

But the three of us still get along really well, even if my

mom is a regular clean-up-your-room-and-do-the-dishes kind of mother. And she is, but she's okay as moms go.

Now we can go back to where I left off. I think I've explained everything I have to, and I can tell you how Lucas helped us figure out a way for my mom to take the job with *The Scene*.

Lucas isn't just smart, she also knows how to handle lots of things. When I told her about the problem with my mom and the job at *The Scene*, she played it cool. Didn't say anything.

Then she went home and did what she'd heard her dad talk about doing before he makes an argument in court: she constructed her case. She says that means you have to find the right arguments to use to talk people into doing what you want them to do.

The next day she went to her mother. Remember how I said Camellia was always wanting to fly off to Santa Fe or wherever? Well, since Lucas and Justin were too old for a nanny and since Allen was away a lot of the time, Camellia had to stay home and take care of the kids—or, actually, the kid. Just Lucas, because Justin was in that private academy. Lucas was old enough to take care of herself, but of course her mom couldn't leave her alone for whole weeks.

So Lucas suggested to her mom that she, Lucas, should go along with Mom and me on our trips during those times I couldn't stay with Uncle Geoff. She could keep me company and help pay expenses. Her mom could be free to run around during the time we were gone. And it would get Lucas out of her dad's hair, which might lower the tension in the household.

*And*, she told her mother, it would give her, Lucas, the chance to see and learn about international culture. She figured that would have real snob appeal for her parents, who go to dinners and parties with people who are all trying to give their children every advantage money can buy and get them into Harvard.

And since my mom would be working as a magazine writer who covered European fashion trends (which, as you can imagine, really appealed to somebody like Camellia), she, Lucas, would be right in the middle of the latest in clothes for young adults, and that might help her have a more fashionable look.

Her mother loved the idea. When it comes to clothes, Lucas and her mom are on whole different planets. On the one hand there's Camellia, who'll go out and spend thousands of dollars on clothes in one day. And on the other there's Lucas, whose idea of dressing up is a clean pair of jeans. Camellia is always telling Lucas she looks like a slob. Actually what she says is that Lucas looks vulgar. Or, as she says it, "vulguh."

And about missing school—Mom could schedule most of our trips during vacations. Lucas said that because these would be international trips, the schools would probably think of them as educational, and because both she and

I are good students, we might be able to take time away from classes if we had to sometimes, as long as we kept up on all our homework.

Well, Lucas's parents bought all her arguments, and they spent one entire evening with Mom having dinner at a restaurant talking about how it would all work. I don't know exactly what they said—they didn't take us along—but they came to an agreement. Problem solved. Mom took the job.

# Camellia's Idea of a Wardrobe

Okay, so the next thing you know, it's March, Mom has had her job with *The Scene* for half a year, and she's already taken three short trips while I stayed with Uncle Geoff twice and Lucas once. Now her bosses have given her so much to do in London that she's going to have to be away for two weeks, and she wants Lucas and me to go along, so in exactly a month, the Gleesome Threesome is leaving for a trip over spring break.

One Saturday afternoon Camellia called. Lucas and I were in my room, and Mom was in the kitchen paying bills. I answered, as usual, and she said, "Hah, Kar-ih."

"Hah" is the way Mrs. Stickney says "hi." I think I told you that she's from the South, and even though she moved here before Lucas was born, she still talks like Scarlett O'Hara in *Gone with the Wind*. Mom always says she thinks Camellia's accent is charming. I'd probably think the same thing if I didn't know it was phony. After fifteen years here, she's really lost her accent, and when nobody special is around—and I haven't been special at Lucas's house since about the third time I stayed overnight—she talks with almost no accent at all. It's plain to Lucas and me that she works hard to talk like a Southerner because she thinks it makes her sound sexy or something. I think she should just give it up.

Anyway, that morning it was obvious she had something in mind, because she was laying the accent on thick. "Hah, Kar-ih, are y'all gonna be home for awhahl?"

"Yeah," I said.

"Well, I thought I'd c'mon over and show y'all the clothes I got this mornin' for Punkin to wear on the trip. Is that all right?"

"Sure," I said. "I guess."

Pumpkin, or Punkin, if you're talking like Scarlett O'Hara, is Camellia's name for Lucas. She says she only let her husband name their little girl Lucas because he's such a bully and he was in such a bad mood anyway because they'd had a girl instead of a boy. The only time she ever calls her daughter Lucas is when she's mad at her or is being what my mom calls *firm and clear*.

"Lucas," I said when I hung up the phone, "did your mom talk to you about clothes to take to Europe?"

"Kind of," Lucas said. "She asked me what I was taking,

and I said mostly jeans and T-shirts and a couple of sweaters. I told her your mom said we had to pack light, and get everything in one of those little suitcases on wheels. But Mom said we'd have to get at least one or two outfits for going out to dinner and things so I won't look 'vulguh.'"

"Well, she's been shopping, and she's coming over."

"Uh-oh," Lucas said. "I'd better take off my glasses."

Lucas has contacts, but she hates putting them in and taking them out, so most of the time she wears her glasses. Camellia thinks Lucas looks better without her glasses, so when she's around, Lucas takes her glasses off and pretends to be wearing her contacts.

I headed for the kitchen to tell Mom.

When I gave her the news, Mom moved her reading glasses down on her nose, looked over them, and raised her eyebrows—it was what Uncle Geoff calls her dry look, which means she doesn't smile, but it's still funny—and said, "This should be interesting." That was all she said, but you could tell she thought it was going to be a disaster, one way or another.

You know how you see people in movies leaving department stores with piles of boxes, but in real life you just get bags? Well, Camellia is the only person I know who actually gets boxes. By the time we'd hauled everything upstairs that Camellia had bought, we had thirty-three boxes, not counting the shoes.

"I was just out at the Mall of America to pick up a few little bitty things, and I saw some clothes I thought would

be just *adorable* for Punkin," she said, after Mom had gotten her a mineral water. She was pulling out clothes and
draping them over the couch. "I know how Punkin just
*hates* to go shoppin'."

"I sure do hate to go shopping, Mom," was all Lucas
said. Last year Mom heard her being snotty to her mother
after Camellia had been on one of her Lucas shopping
sprees. Mom told Lucas that there are lots of ways to say
"I love you." Some people do it by tucking you in at night,
and some people do it by buying clothes for their little
girl. Mom said these shopping sprees were Camellia's way
of saying "I love you." So now when Camellia buys clothes
for Lucas, Lucas is nice to her.

Camellia must have loved Lucas a lot this time, because
the clothes just went on and on.

She started out with the casual things she knew Lucas
would at least think about wearing, like jeans, khakis,
T-shirts, and sweaters. After she finished with the first
bunch, she moved into the noncasual clothes. Blouses.
Dresses. Skirts. There was even a black leather outfit.
("'Cause I always think leather looks so European, don't
you, Gillian?")

Our living room and dining room are kind of one big
space, and by this time she was hanging things over the
dining room chairs. Every time she moved on to another
chair I'd want to look at Lucas, but I knew I'd better not
or I'd burst out laughing.

As if all the clothes and shoes weren't enough, there

was an entire three-section hanging case full of travel-sized cosmetics. There was even a little jar of eye-makeup remover pads, as if Lucas would ever wear eye makeup.

Then Camellia picked up the last box. "Gillian, I want you to know, I got the idea for this gorgeous thing from that last "London Looks" you did in *The Scene*. In the January magazine? 'Member?" Then with a lot of drama she pulled off the cover of the box and whipped out two bright-colored saris.

I am not kidding. Saris.

One was turquoise, and one was lemon yellow. Even my mom, who had been oohing and aahing in encouragement throughout the fashion show so far, was speechless.

I should explain that part of Mom's job, when she goes to a city abroad, is to work with a photographer to take pictures of actual people she sees on the street who she thinks look stylish. Then they're published in what's called the "Looks" section.

Sure enough, "London Looks" had included a picture of two beautiful Indian or Pakistani girls wearing saris, only instead of draping them over their shoulders, they'd wrapped them around their waists.

"I bought one for each of you kids," Camellia said, holding both saris out. To go with them she had found tight-fitting long-sleeved T-shirts that matched the two colors perfectly. "And I got a kohl pencil just like the ladies from India use to put those lines 'round their eyes."

This time Lucas and I did look at each other, and I swear I almost lost it. I knew we were both thinking how we'd look if we went walking around London wearing saris and black eyeliner.

And to carry all this stuff? One of the hugest suitcases I had ever seen. Black leather. With wheels.

When she was finished, Camellia said, "Now Punkin, honey, I know how much you hate tryin' things on, but do somethin' nice for your mama and try on this little dress." She picked up a really cool V-necked green polka-dot dress. "I want to see how that green looks on you."

Lucas shot a glance at my mother, who gave her a very stern look back, and she got up off the floor where she was sitting. (We all were, since there were clothes on every piece of furniture.) Camellia handed her the dress and a bra (Lucas hates wearing a bra). Then, after hesitating a minute, Camellia followed Lucas into my bedroom carrying a pair of pantyhose, a pair of killer green satin low-heeled shoes, a crystal heart necklace, and the cosmetic case.

Mom and I just looked at each other.

# Splitting Up the Loot

Now, it's important to know that Mom likes to travel light. Ex-treeemly light. No matter how long she's going to be gone, she never takes more than her big purse, the bag with her computer and work papers, and one wheelie suitcase.

We'd already bought a suitcase just like hers for me, and we'd talked about what I was going to take, which was mostly jeans and T-shirt kind of stuff, with a nice outfit for going to a play or a good restaurant.

Now this.

I finally said, "There's enough stuff here for seven trips."

"Honey," Mom said, "there's enough stuff here to outfit the entire audience of teenage girls at your average rock concert."

"What are we going to do?" I said. "Lucas can't take all this stuff along."

"Of course she can't," Mom said. "Don't worry. We'll just leave most of it here. How will Camellia ever know?" She winked at me.

It was a good ten minutes before Lucas and her mom came out of the bedroom, and when they did I almost couldn't believe what I was seeing. There was Lucas, only she didn't look like Lucas at all.

You should have seen her. Was she ever pretty! Her skin seemed to glow and her hair gleamed when she was wearing that dress! Her mom had fluffed her curls out. She was wearing some light-colored lipstick, a little blush, and some mascara. She hardly ever wears any makeup at all, so this was really a change. It hadn't been long since she'd gotten her braces off, so her teeth were all white and straight, and with the eye makeup and no glasses, her eyes looked really big.

"Wow!" I said.

"You look beautiful, Lucas," Mom said.

Knowing Lucas, I thought she'd be embarrassed to be dressed up like that and have everybody looking at her, but she actually looked kind of excited and happy.

"Doesn't she look *gorgeous?*" Camellia said, and her eyes positively sparkled when she looked at her daughter. "That color is so good with your skin and your strawberry blond hair, Punkin." I guess *strawberry blond* is another way of saying *reddish blond*.

Then she turned to us. "I wish her daddy could see her. He'd be so proud."

I personally thought Lucas's dad should be proud of her for a lot of other things besides the way she looked. But I had to admit, even a male chauvinist pig like Allen the Meep would be proud of a daughter who looked as pretty as Lucas did.

"Now Kari, honey," Camellia said, "if there's somethin' here that you like specially, you just go ahead and wear it. I'm sure Punkin won't mind. And Gillian, if there's some-thin' here that's just not *raht*"—she meant *right*—"we'll take it back. I left all the tags on.

"And Lucas, honey, I don't want any argument." She used the name Lucas, so we all knew she was serious. "I want to see pictures of you *in* London, *in* these clothes. We can't have you runnin' around a cosmopolitan city lookin' *vulguh*."

So much for leaving most of the clothes behind.

"Thanks for coming and bringing Lucas's things, Camellia," my mom said. "They're all really lovely. And Lucas does look just—incredibly pretty."

Lucas blushed.

"Mah pleashuh, shugah," Camellia said. "Bah-bah."

When she'd gone, Lucas said, "I've got to put in my con-tacts." She almost ran to her overnight case in the bedroom. When her contacts were in, she went to the full-length mirror in my mom's room. All three of us stood around looking at her reflection.

"You are a lovely young woman, Lucas," Mom said.

"Whah, fiddle-dee-dee, y'all are gonna turn a girl's head," Lucas answered, imitating her mother, but now her eyes were sparkling just like Camellia's had, and her cheeks would have been pink even without the blusher.

At last we went back into the living room and just stared at the stuff. We were all quiet for a minute. Then Lucas said, "What the meep are we going to do?"

Well, we decided to take back everything Lucas hated and the things Mom said were impractical for travel. We saved the clothes that Mom said weren't warm enough for London in April. We'd take them on a summer trip.

Lucas and I are about the same size, so she said, how about if she and I both picked the clothes we were going to wear from the things we had left? That way more clothes could go over with us without taking up any extra space. So we both took things like a jacket, jeans, khakis, tops, sweaters, and comfortable shoes.

I took a black skirt and a crinkly white blouse that had long sleeves and French cuffs, and some shiny black shoes with straps—Camellia had called them "mary janes." I loved the whole outfit, and it looked good with my black hair. Lucas, of course, took the dress she was wearing, which looked spectacular on her, along with the matching shoes and the necklace.

Mom said we could fold up the saris flat. She said that one day when we were in London, the two of us could get dressed up in them and paint the lines around our eyes, take a picture, and get out of our costumes.

Well, there were only a few clothes left: a black blazer, the leather outfit, two sweaters, and a pair of soft leather walking shoes.

"They're all wonderful clothes," Mom said, and sighed, "but I think they look a little too old for you. We'd better take them back, too."

I was bursting with an idea. It really wasn't right that I should say it, because they were Lucas's clothes, not mine. But I couldn't help myself.

"Lucas," I said, "how about if you'd let Mom take them? We could maybe get them in bigger sizes, and they'd all look good on her. And that could be *her* wardrobe. We can take pictures of you in them sitting down, and your mom will never know."

Well, that's what we did. I think it was the coolest travel wardrobe Mom ever had. Maybe the coolest wardrobe she ever had, period.

We decided we'd take the big suitcase back and exchange it for a little one like Mom and I had, plus a small shoulder-type bag for each of us. It was more than Mom was used to taking, but we got everything in.

This all seemed like a disaster at the time. We never guessed that the wardrobe Camellia had bought for us would be used to solve our mystery, and that before our two weeks in London were over, we'd wish we'd brought along not only everything we had, but all the things we'd left behind.

# The Gleesome Threesome in London

Except for that first Gallery Guy part, our adventure began on our fourth day in London.

We were staying with our friend Robert, whom we met when he came to America to visit Uncle Geoff. He used to be an actor, but now he owns a restaurant.

We love Robert and his friend Celia, who says she's really an actress cleverly disguised as an office worker. Celia has blond hair and she's very stylish and good-looking. Robert is a big, friendly guy who lives in a converted carriage house in a *very* unfashionable part of London called Hackney. Even if you've been to London already, you've never been to Hackney, trust me. Tourists never go there. It's a place where regular people in London live.

When other people go to London, they mostly just see the famous tourist places. We do that, too. But when we stay at Robert's house we also get to see what it's like to live in London. We drink tea and eat fresh scones from the corner bakery, and eat at a little fish-and-chips place where you go up to a counter and order your fish and they give you these incredibly good pieces of fried fish piled with a bunch of french fries in a waxed paper cone. We watch sitcoms on TV that nobody in America has ever seen, and shop at grocery stores with people in Caribbean head-dresses and Indian saris and African robes, and a lot of Muslim women with their heads covered. And when we're going back and forth to Robert's place, we get to take long rides on the subway, which they call the tube or the Underground, and on double-decker buses.

My mom says that when you go to a place just to see what all the other tourists see, you're a tourist. But when you go to a place and see how people live and do things in ways that are different from what we do at home, you're a traveler. I like being a traveler better than being a tourist.

Mom had come to London mostly to do a story on the British Museum, and Lucas and I went there with her on Friday, our first day there. Mom was meeting with people, and she let Lucas and me just explore the museum on our own.

The second day, Mom went back to the museum, and Lucas and I stayed in Hackney watching the BBC and exploring the neighborhood. We also got a chance to start writing in the journals Mom had given us to write about our trips.

On Sunday, Mom, Lucas, Celia, and I went and saw the Changing of the Guard with those guys with the big furry hats outside the palace where the queen lives, and we went to a famous department store called Harrods. Then we went to Madame Tussaud's Wax Museum, where they have incredibly real-looking wax statues of almost every famous person you can imagine, like Princess Di and Elvis and Kate Moss and Johnny Depp.

About the only problem we had up until then was remembering to look the right way when we crossed the street. In England they drive on the left side of the road instead of the right. That feels confusing when you're inside a bus or a taxi. It's also really bad for pedestrians from countries like America where they drive on the right. Like, when I'm home in Saint Paul and go to cross the street, I just automatically look to my left to see what cars might be coming. But in London, if you look left and don't see any cars, you'll probably get run down by the bus coming at you from the right—driving on the left side of the road. It's a miracle more tourists don't get hit by cars.

In fact, one time Lucas almost did. But that comes later.

Sunday is also the day Robert's restaurant is closed. Even though he has to cook a lot in his restaurant he still loves doing it, so he stayed home and cooked something special for dinner.

It was delicious. I think we were eating salmon with

raspberry sauce when we started talking about what Lucas and I were going to do the next day.

"Robert and Celia have things to do tomorrow," Mom said, "and I have to meet with a photographer at nine. I know that's a little early for you two. Do you mind spending another day just hanging around here?"

"Um, Mom," I began, and looked at Lucas for support, "Lucas and I would like to go into London by ourselves."

Mom was so surprised that she just held her forkful of food in the air for a minute. Then she said, "Forget about it," as if the discussion was over, and started eating again.

"Why?"

"Because you're too young to be wandering around London by yourselves," she said after she'd swallowed.

"No we're not," I said. "We could get along fine."

"Look how well we did on our own in the British Museum," Lucas chimed in. "We never got in trouble, and we always met you exactly when we were supposed to."

Mom, suddenly outnumbered two to one, turned to Robert and Celia. "Tell them they're not old enough, you two," she said, and confidently took another bite of her salmon.

But Robert's answer gave her another surprise. "Course they're old enough, Gillian old girl," he said. "They're not kiddies. They're proper young ladies, they are. What d'you think, Cele?"

"Well, actually," Celia said, "I think when I was their age I got along quite nicely in London on my own. But of course I knew my way about." Celia doesn't sound like Robert when she talks. She sounds more like the rich English people that you see in movies.

I came up with a good argument. "We *do* know our way about. I mean around. We're always the ones who tell Mom which way to go on the Underground, and we always find the right bus to catch. And by now we're used to looking right instead of left before we cross the street. And last time we were in London, Mom and I walked all over. I remember exactly how to get to almost all the places we saw, and I know where we can find the public loos. I mean bathrooms. Whatever." *Loo* is the English word for *bathroom.*

"But how about safety?" Mom said. "London attracts some pretty bizarre characters."

"Not in April," Robert said. "We don't start attracting the swarming hordes of bleeding tourists until at least May. It's that lot gives us trouble. We native Londoners are angels. Good Church of England stock."

"Yeah, right," Mom broke in. "Bet you haven't been to church since the day you were christened."

Robert turned to Celia just as if he'd never been interrupted. "What say we let Gillian and these young women use our mobiles?" That's what they call cell phones over there.

"Brilliant," Celia said, and nodded.

"Besides," Robert added, "we don't have more than seven, eight cases a year of young girls being captured and sold into white slavery under Lord Nelson's column." He gave Lucas and me a big wink.

"Please, Mom?" My mom is not one of those mothers who change their mind if their kid whines enough, but I thought a little begging couldn't hurt.

"Why do I have the feeling I've lost control of this argument?" Mom said.

"Why does your mum feel she ever had control of the argument?" Robert said, and gave Lucas and me a second wink.

So we spent the rest of the night getting about a billion instructions from Mom. She said we should call her every hour. Plus she told us don't talk to strangers, stay together, always stop and look at which way the cars are coming before you cross the street, be polite to everyone, etcetera, etcetera.

She did *not* say, "And if a mystery pops up right in front of your face, stay out of it." Which was a good thing. Because the next day we stepped right into the middle of a mystery, and we could start solving it with a clear conscience.

# Go A-way

Here's another place the story begins: in the National Gallery.

Lucas and I were supposed to meet Mom at the National Gallery entrance at five thirty. We chose to meet there because it's in the middle of London on a place called Trafalgar Square, right across from the Lord Nelson column Robert had talked about. By the way, Lord Nelson is the guy who led the Battle of Trafalgar, where the English navy defeated Napoleon. If you're interested in that kind of thing.

Anyway, we were having a totally cool time. First I showed Lucas the Tower of London, which is an old, old castle kind of place with teeny slits for windows and a stone wall around it. Famous people used to have their heads chopped off there in the olden days, including a couple of the wives of Henry VIII. While we were there we also went into the part where they keep the Crown Jewels, which are the crowns and things that all the kings and queens of England have worn for hundreds of years. You wouldn't believe how many diamonds there are on the main crown they use these days, or how big the diamonds are and how they sparkle.

After the Tower of London we found a McDonald's. Mom had told us that the menu at McDonald's is different in different countries. She was right. I had a Toasted Deli Sandwich Chicken Salad on a brown roll and an Orange Matchmakers McFlurry. Then we went to Piccadilly Circus, which is not a circus at all. I guess *circus* is an old word for a ring or circle, and this is a circle right in the middle of town that's kind of like Times Square in New York only with smaller buildings and not as many signs. We went to a few stores and scoped out the boys. We decided most of them looked just like the guys from Minnesota.

We planned to keep walking around central London all day and not get to the National Gallery until the last minute, but it started to rain, and the museum isn't far from Piccadilly Circus, so we got there early.

In America, the word *museum* can mean a place where they have a collection of almost anything, or a place where they mostly have art. But in England, places where they have just art are usually called galleries. So the National

Gallery is a place where they just have art. We still called it a museum most of the time, because that's what it seemed like to us. Besides, it's kind of confusing, because *gallery* is also another name for a room inside the museum.

Anyway, like I said, the National Gallery is full of nothing but art, mostly thousands and thousands of old paintings. So we started looking at the paintings, just to pass the time. I actually like a lot of old paintings, but after I've seen a few hundred of them, the only way I can possibly not be bored is to try to look for funny things in them.

A lot of the people in paintings are naked, and if you try to have a sense of humor when you look at them, you suddenly see that they're doing all sorts of weird things, like riding horses and tending sheep and having picnics together in the country and talking to angels, all without any clothes on. If you look at the paintings that way, a lot of them are really funny.

So Lucas and I went from room to room laughing and having a great time, until we got to the Rembrandt room.

One of the things that's cool about the paintings by Rembrandt is that there are kind of darkish parts, and then there are parts that look like there's a light shining on them, and Rembrandt was able to make that happen just by using paint. I love that. Also I've painted enough to know how hard that is, so I wanted to look at all his pictures carefully to see how he did it.

But Lucas isn't as crazy about them as I am, and it wasn't long before she seemed to be more interested in a man who was sitting on a stool with an easel, copying from a big painting called *Belshazzar's Feast*, which takes up most of a whole wall at the end of the room. She was trailing along with me, but she kept turning around and looking over at him, obviously trying to see his work. He was sitting just a few inches away from his easel, blocking the view of what he was painting. I kept going around the room looking at one painting after the other and not paying much attention.

It just so happened that we were standing in front of one of the paintings close to *Belshazzar's Feast* and Lucas was still glancing at the guy painting at the easel when all of a sudden this bratty ten-year-old boy breaks away from the school group he's with, comes up really close to the man, and tries to peek between him and the canvas he's working on. Lucas says the painter actually reached out and shoved the kid away. My back was turned so I didn't see it, but I heard what he said to the kid plain as day.

You guessed it. He snarled, "Go a-*way*."

I turned around. In fact, I probably spun around. I could only see the side of the man's head, but he must have been giving the boy the world's dirtiest look, because the kid was moving backward across the room, his eyes huge, like he was scared.

My heart was pounding about twice as fast as usual,

and I felt like my face had turned bright red. For some reason I had the feeling that Lucas and I had to get out of there before the man turned around and recognized us from when he'd seen us in Minneapolis.

I did almost the same thing I'd done when we'd been there with him in the Art Institute. Trying to seem as cool as I could, I walked over, grabbed tight on Lucas's arm, and pulled until she started walking with me out of the room.

Once out, Lucas wanted to stop, but I kept walking, holding on to her arm and almost dragging her until, half-way through the next room, she gave up and fell into step beside me.

"What are you doing?" she said. "Where are you going?" But I didn't answer her. I didn't even look at her. I just walked fast, zigzagging through a bunch of rooms of paintings until I figured that if the guy left the Rembrandt room for any reason, there was no way he was going to find us. Then I dropped onto a bench in the middle of a very crowded and noisy gallery, and Lucas sat down beside me.

"It's him," I said.

"Him who?"

"Him the man we saw in the Art Institute painting the *Lucretia*s. Remember? I went up to look at his easel and he said, 'Go a-*way*,' just like that guy just did. We called him Gallery Guy."

First Lucas looked blank, and then all of a sudden her face changed.

"Gallery Guy! I remember now," she said. "He *did* sound the same. But he doesn't look the same. Didn't the man in the Art Institute have gray hair?"

I nodded. "Back then he didn't look anything like he does now. He had a gray ponytail. And I'm almost sure he didn't wear glasses. And when he was in Minneapolis he was wearing something scruffy, like an old flannel shirt and jeans." The guy we'd just seen had slicked-back dark hair, a dark beard, and a mustache. He wore a nice black shirt tucked into black trousers, loafers, and trendy glasses. The one thing the two men had in common was that they both had broad shoulders and looked like they'd be tall if they stood up.

"It must be a coincidence," Lucas said.

I looked at the gazillion people milling around near our bench and lowered my voice. "What do you think the chances are that two totally different men would be copying paintings by the same artist, and when someone went up to look at their work they would say, 'Go a-*way*,' just like that guy did? Huh?"

She looked up and stared at a corner of the ceiling—sometimes she does that when she's thinking—but this time she sat that way for what seemed like a long time.

"Earth to Lucas, Earth to Lucas," I said at last.

She turned back to me. "I was just trying to think of

what that man in Minneapolis would look like if I drew him with dark, slicked-back hair and a beard. You're right, it *is* the same guy," she said.

I thought I'd stopped being surprised by Lucas's photographic memory, but it seemed incredible that even after more than a year, she could just think back about the man we'd called Gallery Guy and remember what he looked like so perfectly that she could have drawn him. I was also totally glad I wasn't the only one thinking there was a connection between the men we'd seen in the two museums.

I didn't want to show her how impressed I was, or how much it meant to me to have her agree with me. So I just said, "See, I knew it was the same guy!" Then I added, "I wonder . . ."

"What he's doing that makes him think he has to wear a disguise?" Lucas finished for me.

"Uh-huh."

Now we were both quiet for a minute. "What are you thinking?" I asked finally. She had an expression I'd seen before.

"Oh, nothing."

"Nothing my meep. When you get that look, it usually means you're making some plan that's going to get us in trouble."

"No, no, nothing like that," she said, trying to sound all innocent.

But I was right. She *was* planning something. In fact, that afternoon in the National Gallery was the beginning of something that would get us into more trouble—and put the whole Gleesome Threesome in more danger—than we'd ever been in before.

# Keeping the Truth from Mom

I looked at my watch. "It's almost five thirty already. Mom's going to be here in a minute."

We got up from where we were sitting and headed for the front steps, where we were supposed to meet her.

I was still worried about what Lucas was thinking. I figured it had to do with Gallery Guy, and I had a really bad feeling about him. "I want to stay away from that man," I said as we walked into the next room. "He might recognize us."

"From the Art Institute?"

I nodded.

"Are you nuts? He must chase away kids who are trying to look at his canvas all the time. How could he remember all of them? Besides, think about how different we look now than we did then."

She was right that we'd changed a lot. In the last year both of us had gotten our braces off, Lucas had grown about two inches, and we'd both gotten—well, not big boobs exactly, but a more womanly shape, as they say. I'd cut my hair to just below shoulder length, and I'd stopped wearing glasses and started wearing contacts.

"But you remembered his face well enough to know it was the same guy even with his disguise. What if he has a photographic memory, too?"

"Not many people do. Probably not more than one in a thousand. And besides, what if he did recognize us? It's not like seeing him in both places is against the law or anything."

"I'm not so sure about him needing a photographic memory to remember us. My dad doesn't have a photographic memory, but he's painted enough portraits that he has a good memory for faces. Besides, there's something about that guy that just creeps me out. He's mean."

"You're right. Even I can tell that." Lucas may be smarter than I am, but I have a lot more intuition than she does, and a lot of the time I feel things that she doesn't. If she felt something was wrong about Gallery Guy, I knew he must be sending off some scary vibes.

When we got to the building's big entryway, it had stopped raining. We went outside and hung over the railing at the top of the entrance steps and looked over Trafalgar Square. Part of the reason we did that was just because it was a great view: the square with its pigeons and tourists, the huge, enormous column with the Lord Nelson statue on top of it, the other statues, the big fountain spurting up and landing in a pool, the red double-decker buses and all the other traffic racing around.

But mostly it was because we hoped if we got out where there were lots of people and hung way over the side of the railing, Gallery Guy wouldn't notice us if he came out before Mom got there. Somehow, although neither of us could explain why, we just didn't want to be noticed.

"I think Gallery Guy is doing something suspicious," Lucas said. She kept her voice low so the people around us couldn't hear.

"I think you're right. But if he is, it's something we don't want to know anything about."

I could have been talking to a wall.

"It's probably even against the law, or he wouldn't be so worried about being recognized. And we're maybe the only people in the entire world who know there's something fishy going on."

I hadn't thought of it that way, and I had to admit, it was pretty cool being one of the only two people who knew that something against the law was happening. Somehow Lucas always finds a way of getting *me* interested in whatever *she's* interested in.

"If we only knew what the crime was," Lucas said. "Let's think. What kind of crimes have to do with art?"

"There's stealing paintings."

"Art theft," Lucas corrected.

"That's what I said. Stealing paintings. He could be, like, planning to . . ."

Suddenly somebody was pressing up behind me, and just for a second I was sure it was Gallery Guy and he was going to push me over the edge. I turned around, but it was only a very overweight man trying to work his way between some other people and me.

I started my sentence over again, still keeping my voice down. "He could be planning to copy a couple Rembrandts, then replace the real ones with his own fakes in museums and sell the real ones."

"That's way complicated," Lucas said. "I think it's more likely he's going to try just plain art forgery, painting something and pretending it was by Rembrandt."

"But why would he need to go to two museums?"

"I don't have a clue. But if what he's doing turns out to be big, we'll probably hear about it. If anything new happens about a Rembrandt painting, the story will probably be in *Time*." Lucas has to read *Time* magazine every week for her social studies class.

"I suppose." It was a relief to think about this. If it was going to be in *Time* magazine, that meant it would be a big, famous story. Lucas and I were just two normal fourteen-year-old girls, so it wouldn't have anything to do with us.

"One thing is for sure, he has something to hide," Lucas said. "If he was doing something normal, he wouldn't be so paranoid about having somebody see what he's doing, and he wouldn't be wearing a disguise."

"Maybe we should ask Mom what he might be up to."

She turned to look at me. "I don't think we should tell your mom about this."

I thought for a minute. "Yeah, she might think it was just one of those kid things."

"Maybe, but your mom has a suspicious mind. I think she might believe something was up, but she'd probably make us promise not to come back here."

"So?"

"We have to come back!" Lucas said. "Tomorrow."

"What do you mean, we have to come back?"

"We have to find out what Gallery Guy is up to. It will be fun, Kari! We've already been to a bunch of tourist places. This will give us something interesting to do."

"You mean, like, spy on Gallery Guy? I don't think that's such a great idea, Lucas. He's not a nice man. Even you think he's mean."

"Hello-o! How much trouble do you think we can get into in the middle of a crowded museum like this? What's he going to do—pull a gun or chase us around with a knife in front of hundreds of people? It will be fun!" she said again.

Suddenly I realized she was right. We'd been to a whole

lot of tourist places, most of which I'd been to when Mom and I were in London before. Most tourist places are more set up for grown-ups than for teenagers, and to be honest, sometimes they're boring. Spying on a guy who might be up to something really big and important did seem way more interesting.

During this whole time, we were so busy with what we were saying that we'd sort of forgotten to look for Mom. Suddenly I felt a tap on my back, which scared the meep out of me, and there she was, standing behind us. I felt like Lucas and I needed more time to figure out how to handle the situation, but we just had to go on the best we could.

"Hi, Mom," I said, trying to smile.

"Hi, guys," she said. "I'm glad to see you survived your day in one piece."

Normally Lucas and I would have made some sarcastic comments, asking her how much trouble she thought we could get into when we had to talk to her on Robert's mobile phone every hour. But I for one was too busy thinking about Gallery Guy to come up with any smart remarks.

Mom squeezed in beside me at the rail. "How was it seeing London on your own?"

"Fine," I said, "just fine." Great conversation I was making.

"We're kind of tired," Lucas said, as if explaining why I couldn't think of anything more original to say. "Why don't you tell us about your day first? How was it? We'll tell you about our day later." Lucas is always cool in a crisis.

"Okay," Mom said, but she raised her eyebrows a little, as if she wasn't sure what was going on. She really does have a suspicious mind.

"How was my day? Well, I'm having a heck of a time. I have a photographer to help me take pictures in the British Museum and we're going to start shooting tomorrow, but I don't like any of the themes I've come up with for the story, so I'm not even sure what we're going to take pictures *of.*"

The National Gallery was about to close, and the landing was getting more and more crowded. A school group had come out behind us, and all these little kids were playing around and jostling us.

I started giving them dirty looks over my shoulder and said, "Mom, could we—" I was going to ask if we could get the meep out of there, when suddenly I saw Gallery Guy coming out the museum door. He didn't have his easel or his painting with him, and he didn't even glance in our direction. I was glad he didn't see us, but having him so close to us still made me nervous.

"You want to go?" Mom said, and turned.

"No!" I said quickly. "I mean, could we just wait here a second?"

Lucas said, "Yeah, we've been inside all afternoon, and just as you came up we were saying how fun it is to look over everything happening on Trafalgar Square. I especially like the buses."

"Sure," Mom said, but I saw her following my eyes as I watched Gallery Guy going down the steps to the sidewalk.

"Who's that?" she asked. "What's going on here?"

"That's just a guy we saw in the Rembrandt room," I said, ignoring her second question. It maybe wasn't the whole truth, but it was the truth and nothing but the truth, and it sounded especially honest coming right after Lucas's lie. I always think it's good to tell the truth to your parents whenever you can. For one thing, it's usually easier.

"You are going to use the mummies, aren't you?" Lucas asked. She was talking about what Mom had said about trying to decide what to feature in her story about the British Museum. They have Egyptian mummies there that Lucas and I really like.

I suppose now is as good a time as any to explain exactly what Mom kept doing in the British Museum. If you read *The Scene*, you've probably seen some of my mom's stories about museums. She did the very first one the other time we went to London. It was about the costumes at the Victoria and Albert Museum, and I guess a lot of kids read it. So since then she's done two more, one on the big Louvre museum in Paris, and one on a museum in Florence, Italy.

Mom talked the people at *The Scene* into letting her do

four museum stories a year. She's always telling me she's so tired of articles on supermodels that she could just throw up, and if the magazine doesn't try to do something for the 999 girls out of a thousand who could never be models, she doesn't think they're being very responsible. So she tries to get them to run articles that help get girls interested in things besides just their looks and boys.

Anyway, it was time for *The Scene* to run another museum story. This one was going to be about the British Museum. So that's mostly what she had to do in London this time, besides another "London Looks." All the time we'd been in London, she'd been trying to find a theme for her article and decide what to have the photographer take pictures of.

Lucas's question about the mummies had been just the right thing to get Mom started.

"Yeah, I'm definitely going to include them. I figure if you're that interested in them, other kids will be, too. In fact, maybe—" She broke off. "Oh, duh. Good grief. Why didn't I think of it before? How about, 'The British Museum: A Teenager's Guide'?"

"Sounds like a good theme to me," I said, though I actually thought it seemed pretty basic.

"Of course! That's it!" Mom said. "I'll take you two around to the galleries tomorrow and we'll take pictures of whatever you're the most interested in."

I saw Lucas's face fall, and even I felt disappointed.

So much for our plans to come back and keep an eye on Gallery Guy.

Mom was too excited with her idea to notice. "I've been racking my brain for almost a week. You'd think I'd have thought of something so obvious at least four days ago. Terrific! I suddenly feel all energized."

I looked at Lucas. It was obvious she didn't feel all energized, and neither did I.

# Blessings Upon Thee, O Camellia

We were going to eat at Robert's restaurant that night. The restaurant isn't as far away from central London as Robert's house, but it still takes a long time to get there on a double-decker bus. When we got on, Lucas and I went to find a place to sit upstairs. We never got tired of sitting upstairs on double-decker buses and noticing how weird it felt to drive on the left side of the road.

"We've got to figure out something so we can get back to the National Gallery tomorrow," Lucas said the minute we were away from Mom.

"Well, the only thing I can think of that would keep us out of the British Museum completely would be a bomb scare," I said, "and I think that might be going a little bit far."

"Yeah, probably a bit," Lucas said with a sigh, as if she was sad to give up the idea. "But let's at least make out a list tonight of our favorite things in the British Museum. We'll show them to your mom as fast as we can tomorrow morning, and maybe by the time we've had lunch, we'll be able to go check out what Gallery Guy is doing."

"Good thinking," I said. "And sometime tonight I'll let her know we have our own plans for the afternoon and don't want to be stuck in the British Museum all day."

So we pulled out the little tablet Lucas used for a sketch pad and one of her soft lead drawing pencils and started making our list.

On the bus I'd been thinking I'd absolutely hate the time we had to spend in the restaurant, because I wanted to be talking to Lucas about our plans for the next day. But believe it or not, when we actually got there, there were so many other things to think about that I almost totally forgot about Gallery Guy.

Mom and I had met the chef and one of the waitresses the last time we were in London, and this was the first time we'd eaten there on this trip, so everybody kept coming over to our table and making a fuss over us, and bringing over tall nonalcoholic drinks with pieces of fruit on little sticks.

What with everything going on, I forgot all about Gallery Guy until we were in the middle of the meal. When I did remember him, I got a little shiver of excitement thinking about being in the gallery with him again, even though I was still worried that he'd remember us from that time in Minneapolis. Then I thought of something that totally spoiled my appetite.

What if Gallery Guy remembered us from Minneapolis and *also* happened to look at us yesterday when we weren't watching him? He'd recognize us right away and figure out we were spying on him. Even though we had a right to be in the museum, I had the feeling he'd find some way to make sure we didn't find out what he was up to. The thought gave me the shivers.

"Aren't you going to finish the rest of your chicken?" Mom asked as I arranged my silverware on my plate. "I thought you said it was delicious."

"It is. But I'm full."

"Well, you're going to have to eat more of it than that if you want dessert," she said. Typical. I knew what desserts were like at Robert's, so I shoved in a few more mouthfuls.

Mom had been asking where we'd gone before the National Gallery, and Lucas was telling her all about the Tower of London.

While they talked, I was in my own private world, thinking about how to spy on Gallery Guy without having him recognize us. Then I thought of another thing: the guard.

If you go to museums, you know there are usually guards in uniforms hanging around, keeping an eye on all that expensive artwork. Well, the Rembrandt room had one of those guards. A balding guy. I'd noticed him right away because he had such a prissy expression. He had a long, pointed nose, and he held it high up in the air and looked down over it to let you know that he thought he was better than everybody else. He stood by the door scoping out everybody who came and went.

What if he saw us hanging around, trying to see what Gallery Guy was working on? Would he make us leave the museum? Would he tattle to Gallery Guy? That gave me the shivers again.

Then I came up with an idea. I don't want to brag, but I think it was pretty brilliant.

Disguises.

Even after we'd weeded out the clothes Camellia had bought, we still had enough clothes to disguise ourselves as most of the Justin Timberlake fans from an average ninth-grade class. Plus there was that whole three-section bag full of cosmetics.

What's more, Camellia had provided us with the perfect excuse to use them all.

I waited until Lucas had stopped telling Mom about what they had on the McDonald's menu.

"You know, one thing we haven't done yet is to get any pictures of Lucas in those clothes Camellia wanted her to wear. Maybe we should take a couple of outfits along tomorrow, and after we've finished at the British Museum"—I kicked Lucas under the table—"we could go get some shots at Trafalgar Square. We could take the tube and bus back to Robert's when we're done."

"Sounds okay to me." Relief, relief, she didn't expect us to stay with her all day long. "But where would you change?"

"We could change in the museum bathroom where we went this afternoon. It's way in the back, in the part of the building where they have classes. We went twice and there wasn't anybody else around either time." This was absolutely true, and what was *really* great was that this quiet little bathroom was close to the Rembrandt room.

"Well, okay, but you're going to have to make a list of everything you have along so you don't forget anything."

Lucas hadn't said a word during all of this, but I'd seen by her expression that she'd at least half figured out what I had in mind about the disguises. When mom went off to the restroom, I explained it all.

"Is it brilliant, or what?" I said when I'd finished explaining.

"Definitely brilliant," she answered.

Then, folding her hands and looking toward heaven, she said, "Blessings upon thee, O Camellia. God, I take back everything bad I've ever said about my mother."

She looked down, then looked back up again. "Well, maybe not quite everything."

# 12

# "Watchit, Dad"

There was just one more thing that happened in the restaurant that turned out to be important later. Before we left, Celia dropped in to join us, and somebody else took over behind the bar so Robert could come sit at our table.

It's always fun when Robert and Celia are around. Celia's cool, and when we're with her we all like to tease Robert, who teases us right back.

So when Celia saw Robert walking over to our table, she whispered to us, "After a few minutes, ask Robert if he's ever had a part in a movie. And keep asking him until he tells you about his lines."

A little while after he sat down, Lucas said, sounding casual, "Have you ever been in a movie, Robert?"

"Once," he said. "Thing called *Streets of Fear*. Yes, I remember it well. Didn't go very far. Should have done better, what with me having a speaking role."

"What did you play?" I asked.

"A young tough," Robert said. "Black leather jacket, a spiderweb tattooed on one cheek."

"So what did you say in the movie?" Lucas asked.

"I'm not sure I can remember. . . ."

"Oh, Robert," Celia said, sounding innocent, "I'm sure you can remember all your lines. In fact, *I* can even remember all your lines. Why don't you tell these sweet girls?"

"Sweet girls my . . . backside. Bunch of ruddy females," he muttered, looking at the four of us. "Okay, you want to know my part, I'll tell you. I said, 'Watchit, Dad.'"

Lucas and I waited. Finally Lucas said, "That's all?"

"Whad'ya mean, that's all? It was an important line, and I delivered it with sensitivity."

Lucas and I looked at each other and rolled our eyes.

"See, I was this young bast— this young ne'er-do-well racing through the streets of London on a motorcycle, and I ran over an old bloke who couldn't get out of my way, and as he lay dying on the street I looked down on him and said, 'Watchit, Dad.'"

"Was the man really your dad? In the movie, I mean?" I asked.

"Naaow." (That's how Robert says *no.*) "See, in England, young people without manners, *like you lot,* call older blokes 'Dad,' the way the posh crowd might call them 'Sir.'"

I leaned toward him and shoved him with my elbow. "Watchit, Dad," I said.

"You can't even say it right." So for a few minutes Robert taught Lucas and me how to say "Watchit, Dad," as if we were East Enders, with Celia shaking her head the whole time.

"With that phrase and a black leather jacket, you'll pass for a Londoner anytime," Robert said. "Specially if you hang a ring through your eyebrow."

As it turned out, two days later, one of us did just that.

# Rags, Treasures, and the Women's Loo at the National Gallery

The same kind of thing that had happened at the restaurant happened again the next morning. We'd thought being in the British Museum with Mom would be a real bummer, and we just wanted to get it over with. But it turned out to be pretty good.

The big thing was that we were dressed in some of the new clothes Camellia had bought. My outfit was the black skirt and the crinkly white blouse with the big cuffs. Having a new outfit always makes me feel special.

Even Lucas seemed to like wearing her green polka-dot dress. A person couldn't help noticing again that it was a perfect color for her. And because she knew she looked good in it, she looked even better, if you know what I mean.

We were dressed up because we were going to have our

pictures taken for the magazine. That meant we also had to get all made up by Mom, and that was also cool. Mom said if she'd thought about having us in the pictures ahead of time, she would have gotten a professional makeup artist, and that would have *really* been fun, but since they weren't going to be close-up shots, it didn't have to be a perfect job. After Mom was finished with us, we were wearing more makeup than either of us had ever worn in our lives. We even had on eyebrow pencil and lip liner. We both looked very grown-up and sophisticated, or at least I thought so.

The museum itself was another reason why we ended up having a good morning. Of all the museums I've seen so far, the British Museum is my favorite. Lucas loves it, too. They have Viking stuff, ancient jewelry from almost everywhere you can think of, probably the best collection of coins in the whole world, and room after room of things British explorers brought back from Egypt. And that's only about one-millionth of what they have.

That morning it was especially exciting because we were there before opening time and had it all to ourselves.

We had to pose in the big room with the Parthenon Sculptures, which are beautiful statues and wall carvings of gods and goddesses that some English guy took away from the ruins of a famous temple in Athens, Greece. Mom especially wanted to write a story about it because I guess the Greeks want all the statues back, and there's a big fight about it.

It's funny how being almost alone in that room made me feel. When I'd been crowded in there with enough tourists to about populate the entire state of Ohio, the statues and carvings were just interesting things to look at for a while before we went into another room to look at a few *more* things.

But now that there were way more gods and goddesses than there were people, the statues seemed different. All of a sudden I realized they'd been around for centuries and centuries, and they'd still be there after I died, and after my children and grandchildren and great-great-great-grandchildren died. They're permanent, and we're all only temporary. It was a weird feeling, but it made me glad I'd decided to be an archeologist when I grow up. Uncle Geoff says that's the kind of feeling he gets when he finds something old, and that's what archeology is all about.

Anyway, we posed for a while, which was mostly boring and made us feel silly, especially when ten o'clock came and tourists started pouring into the room. Then we went through the museum with just Mom and the photographer and pointed out our other favorite things. Every place we went, we had to say why we liked what we were showing them, and Mom recorded what we said and took notes to use when she wrote the article.

Then it was lunchtime. And finally, at exactly 1:50, we were free.

We didn't waste any time. We grabbed the bags we'd

packed with our extra clothes, raced across this little park to the tube station, hopped on the next train, and ended up at the entrance to the National Gallery at 2:19. We'd probably set a new speed record.

We were feeling really good about this until we walked into the museum. That's where the problems started.

First a guard stopped us and wouldn't let us in with our backpacks. They want everybody to leave their big bags in the cloakroom before they go in to see the paintings.

I'd never thought of that, and I thought this meant we were completely meeped. But leave it to Lucas. She said, "We're here to take a class. I think we came in the wrong door. You can look—all we have in our bags is clothes. It's a class in fashion drawing." She gestured with her head to where I was standing. "I'm going to draw her in some different outfits, and she's going to draw me."

I held my breath. But the guard said, "I'll take a look, if you don't mind."

He opened both bags, dug around, and finally came up with the expensive digital camera Lucas's parents had given her for the trip. "No cameras."

Lucas and I looked at each other. We were going to use it to take pictures of Gallery Guy and whatever he was doing. There went our entire plan.

The guard must have thought we were upset because we didn't know what to do with our camera while we were in class. "You can still go in," he said. "Put your clothing in one of your bags and I'll let you take that one in. But you'll have to put the camera in the other bag and leave it in the cloakroom."

"Okay." Lucas sounded as discouraged as I felt.

"You know where you're going when you're done checking your bag?"

We nodded.

"Next time, use the education entrance around the other side. More convenient for you."

"I can't believe you got by with that," I said when we left the guard. "How did you know they'd be giving classes in fashion drawing?"

"I didn't." Lucas flopped her backpack onto an empty bench and sat down next to it. "I just figured the guards are in a different department from education, and they probably wouldn't know anything about the classes. Basically we lucked out." Nerves of steel, I tell you.

"What are we going to do without the camera?" She looked at me and I looked at her. For once she didn't have a suggestion.

I sighed. "I guess we'll think of something."

Eventually we got to the deserted women's room practically just downstairs from the Rembrandt room. There wasn't much counter space, so we piled our stuff in one of the sinks. "How different do you think I look?" Lucas said. We were excited again, and this was maybe the seventeenth time one of us had said this.

The day before, when we'd first visited the Rembrandt room, Lucas and I had both been wearing jeans and long-sleeved T-shirts. Lucas had been wearing her glasses—surprise, surprise—and had her hair up in a scrunchy. She'd looked fourteen. Now, in her dress, her contacts, and all the makeup, I thought she looked eighteen, at least. Maybe even twenty.

"You know, the good thing about that dress," I said, not actually answering her question, because I'd already answered it a bunch of times that day, "is that it makes you look all feminine and, uh . . ."

"Kind of harmless, you mean."

"Right. Now if you can just keep your eyes closed, so Gallery Guy doesn't see that you're really a lion inside."

"Just call me Simba. *Rrrraaah.*"

"Simba needs some blush."

"I think I look way younger than you," Lucas said while she put blush on her cheeks with the big, expensive brush Camellia had sent along. "I can't believe how old you look."

I'd pulled my hair back into a smooth ponytail and put on some little pearl earrings.

Lucas said, "You look like a girl who just graduated from college and has her first job in some ritzy company."

"Do you think Gallery Guy will think I look like somebody who has a job, or will he just think I look like a fourteen-year-old wearing too much makeup?"

"With any luck he won't notice you. Don't be nervous. What's he going to do if he does notice us? Track us out of the museum and push us in front of a bus?"

She meant it to sound sarcastic. But when she said it, I suddenly felt afraid. Maybe it was a premonition.

# 14

## Bert

There Gallery Guy was, sitting where he'd been sitting the day before, bent over whatever he was copying from *Belshazzar's Feast* but looking around him every once in a while like it was the most natural thing in the world. There Lucas and I were in the doorway between Gallery 23, what we called the Rembrandt room, and Gallery 24.

A few minutes before, Lucas had figured out what we could use to substitute for the camera, and now we were totally prepared, with our new clothes and makeup and hairdos making us look nothing like we'd looked the day before.

And there, standing almost directly across from us between the Rembrandt room and the entrance to Gallery 22, was the guard, Bert. We found out the next day that that was his name, when one of the other guards walked by him and said, "Afternoon, Bert." But I might as well call him by his name right to begin with.

*Belshazzar's Feast* was at one end of the room. Gallery Guy was back and off to the left of center if you were looking at the painting. There was a bench smack in the middle of everything, and both the exit doors were close to the other end of the room. So with people coming and going the way they do in art galleries, we thought we'd go through the Rembrandt room over and over again as long as Gallery Guy didn't turn around and notice us, and as long as we managed to fool Bert.

Were we going to be able to do it? I wasn't sure. My heart was pounding so hard I wondered if the two guys could hear it.

If you were a complete stranger and didn't know anything about who Lucas and I and the other people were, this is what you would have seen if you'd been there that afternoon.

About a quarter past three, a young woman walked into Gallery 23. She had curly, strawberry blond hair, and was wearing a green polka-dot dress and green shoes. She didn't use the entrance where the museum guard was standing. Instead she came in from the door on the other side of the room.

She was studying a copy of *A Room-to-Room Guide to the National Gallery* that she'd bought in the gift shop, and when she came through the door her head was down as if she was busy reading. As she walked by the first few pictures, she made little notes in the book with a pencil.

The guard never saw the face of the young woman in the green dress because somehow she always managed to have her back to him or her head down in her book. And she didn't seem to have the slightest interest in the paintings hanging near where he was standing.

Just outside the same entrance the girl in green had used was another young woman. She was standing where she couldn't be seen either by the man guarding the Rembrandt room or by the man who was busy copying one of Rembrandt's paintings. She had dark hair, wore a black skirt and crinkly white shirt, and was watching the first young woman carefully.

She noticed that the young woman in green stood for a long time in front of a painting called *Belshazzar's Feast* and slightly behind a man painting at an easel. And though the head of the girl in green was lowered as if she was really interested in her guidebook, her eyes were actually looking toward the painter's canvas. Whenever she glanced over in that direction, she'd look back and make another note in the guidebook. When the artist turned around—probably because he felt someone looking at him—the young woman was slightly turned away from him, studying her book again.

After one last glance over the painter's shoulder, the young woman in green left the Rembrandt room and

walked into the gallery where the other young woman was
waiting.

Five minutes later the young woman in the black skirt
and white shirt walked into the Rembrandt room. She,
too, kept her back toward the guard standing at the central entrance. Eventually, after she'd spent a lot of time
standing behind the guy painting at the easel, and looking
at the pictures that hung near the one called *Belshazzar's
Feast*, she sat down on the bench in the room and pulled
some postcards from a bag she'd gotten at the gift shop.
Keeping her head down, she appeared to be writing on
the postcards. Then she put the postcards back in the gift
shop bag, wandered over behind the painter again, then
went out of the room the way she'd come in.

Later, two girls who looked and acted about twelve
or thirteen came into the gallery together. Both girls had
their hair pulled back in buns like ballet dancers have. One
of the girls had a silver retainer on her teeth. The other
one wore glasses.

The girl with the reddish blond hair was dressed in
jeans and a long-sleeved T-shirt. The other girl was wearing a green sweater with black pants. As they stood looking at the painting around the corner from the one called
*Belshazzar's Feast,* the first girl was whispering to the second girl in French about a boy she liked at school. While
the strawberry blonde whispered, the brunette was glancing over the shoulder of the man who was painting at an

easel. As the man turned to look at them, the two started giggling at what the first girl said, and ran into the next gallery.

A half hour before the museum closed, a group of German tourists was taking a guided tour through the National Gallery. When they got as far as the Rembrandt room, the guide, speaking in German, stopped in front of one of two Rembrandt self-portraits. Toward the back of the group, wearing a sweater, tight jeans, and a jeans jacket, was a brunette with dark hair pulled back in a messy ponytail, a lot of heavy eye makeup, and dark lipstick.

Of all the people in the German group, this young woman was the one standing closest to the man at the easel. When the guide walked to the next room and the tourists began to follow, the young woman seemed to be jostled by someone in front of her. She took a quick step backward, slightly brushing the back of the painter. But as he turned to say something nasty to her, she moved to his other side, where she leaned toward him briefly to say, "Sorry," with a little accent. Then, before he could catch a glimpse of her face, she'd turned and was gone with the rest of the group.

In all that time, Bert never realized that these were all the same two girls.

15

# Oscars and a Fingertip

"We are sooooooo GOOD!" Lucas shouted as we got back to the women's room.

"And for the best performance by an actress . . . may I have the envelope, please," I said into the mirror. I was still wearing my German tourist outfit.

Lucas handed me her *Room-to-Room Guide*, then when I frowned she found my bag of postcards and gave it to me with a flourish.

"And the Oscar goes to . . ." I pulled a postcard from the bag with a huge gesture. "Oh my goodness, there's been a tie! The winners are Lucas Stickney and Kari Sundgren!"

We did the Hollywood thing of "dahling" and kisses on both cheeks.

Lucas picked up a shoe, walked closer to the mirror, and bent her head, as if she was about to talk into a microphone. "We'd like to thank the Academy," she said, holding the shoe as if it were the Oscar, "and we'd like to thank Gillian Welles Sundgren, who made our performance possible. And Mr. Gallery Guy, without whose help we wouldn't be here this evening."

She looked at me and bit her lip, as if she knew there were more people to thank, but she'd forgotten who they were. She was totally getting into this.

I whispered to her.

"And Camellia Stickney for supplying the costumes, and Rembrandt, and *The Scene* magazine. Oh, and a guard at the National Gallery in London, who inspired our performance."

She stepped aside, still holding Oscar. I approached the invisible mike with the other shoe.

"And we'd like to thank our families, except for Allen the Meep and the Brat Child, who don't deserve thanks for anything." We'd just watched the Academy Awards a few weeks before and I'd seen some guy talking about some political thing until he had to be almost shoved off the stage, so I added, "And while I'm at the microphone, I'd like to call the Academy's attention to the continuing problem of discrimination against people who wear size eight shoes. . . ."

Lucas cracked up.

We'd promised each other we wouldn't let ourselves get too excited until after the whole day was over and we'd managed it all without being found out. Now we let it all loose, and we laughed and hooted and joked around the whole time we were getting back into normal clothes, and all the way down to the tube station where we started our trip back to Robert's house.

After the morning at the British Museum, Mom had gone back to Hackney to do some writing. So together with her we'd plotted out our route home taking the tube and a bus, and she left us on our own with our London Transport passes. She only asked that we call every hour again, and one last time when we were ready to start back so she'd know when to expect us, and we'd done that.

We spent the entire tube ride talking about what had happened—what good actresses we were, how neither Bert nor Gallery Guy seemed to have noticed us, how glad Lucas was that in her stuck-up private school she'd been taking French since third grade, how well I'd managed the German tourist thing, etcetera, etcetera.

Once on the bus, we pulled out what we'd written and drawn. Lucas had her drawing on the inside back cover of her guidebook. I'd used the back of two postcards. We'd drawn everything we'd seen of Gallery Guy's canvas.

But the only thing we'd seen that looked like anything in particular was exactly one fingertip.

That's it. Just a fingertip. It looked like a woman's fingertip. The fingernail side.

I was the one who'd seen it sticking up about six inches

from the top of the canvas. Lucas had seen something that looked like gold, lacy fabric on the left side, and we'd both seen dark red on the right that we thought was like a background or something.

Of course we'd used plain old pencils to make our copies, so nothing was in color.

From what we'd seen, it was hard to figure out what part of Rembrandt's painting Gallery Guy was copying. I suppose I should explain about *Belshazzar's Feast*. It's big, about seven feet wide and as tall as I am. In the middle is this guy in a turban—Belshazzar, from the Bible story. God warned him about something by writing a message to him on the wall when he was surrounded by people, having a holy feast or an orgy or something. You know how people say, "I saw the handwriting on the wall"? Well, Belshazzar was the first one to see the handwriting on the wall. At least that's what it says in the Bible.

In Rembrandt's picture a bunch of people are sitting around a table with grapes on it. (Grapes seem to be big in famous paintings.) Everybody in Rembrandt's picture has clothes on, so it probably wasn't an orgy. Belshazzar is kind of half getting up from his chair, and looking at this mysterious hand coming out of a cloud or some smoke or something, and writing on the wall in a foreign alphabet. Belshazzar and the people around him all look worried.

Well, in Rembrandt's painting there's some red in a woman's dress, but it wasn't the same color red as what I'd seen on the right-hand side of Gallery Guy's canvas. The lacy fabric Lucas had seen on the left side might have come from the cape or shawl thing Belshazzar is wearing.

Then there was the fingertip, which didn't seem to match anything in *Belshazzar's Feast*. You don't notice it unless you're looking for it, but the painting is full of people making gestures with their hands. Trouble was, the fingertip I'd seen was pointed upward—not straight, but up-ish, if you know what I mean. The only fingers pointed even partly upward in Rembrandt's painting are on a woman behind Belshazzar who's holding her hands like you'd do if you were clapping softly and your hands stayed stuck together. Well, it's a little looser than that, but that's kind of it. But even her fingertips weren't pointing upward like the one Gallery Guy had painted. Plus in Rembrandt's painting, those hands weren't really next to the gold on Belshazzar's cape.

God probably knew what Gallery Guy was painting, but we sure didn't.

When we finished comparing what we'd seen, and talking about what Gallery Guy could be working on, we still were a long way from our bus stop, so we began plotting our disguises for the next day.

"Wait," Lucas said, after we'd been talking about disguises for about five minutes. "Let's stay focused on what we want to do here."

"What do you mean?" Focused? We were on a roll.

"What I mean is, why are we doing what we're doing?"

"To find out what Gallery Guy is up to."

"Exactly. We're not here to set some kind of record for getting into the Rembrandt room without being noticed."

"So what do *you* think our next step should be?"

"Here's what I think. I'll draw Gallery Guy sitting in the middle of the room, just like we planned, since we can't use the camera. And we can keep looking at what we can see around the sides of his canvas. But mostly let's just do whatever we can to get a look at what he's painting in the middle, and copy it onto a big canvas, like his."

"Copy the colors? Using what? Oil paints? And where exactly would we set up our canvas? And where would we leave it to dry?" This whole thing sounded like a dumb idea.

"There are some cool starter sets of acrylic paints in the museum gift shop. They dry right away," Lucas said. "And even if you can't reproduce oil paint colors perfectly with acrylic, you can get them pretty close. And we can do it right there. The classes must be on spring break just like our schools at home because it seems like there's never anybody in the loo." We were calling bathrooms "loos" all the time now. It just seemed to come naturally.

"The problem is, you remember what you see and draw better than I do," I said, "but face it: I paint better than you."

"I know. You mix colors better, and you apply them

better, and you're faster, and all that. But we can solve those problems. Let's think about it. Remember, we're soooo GOOD."

When we got back to Robert's, Mom had been watching for us, and she greeted us with the kind of smile that let us know she'd been worried about us coming back alone, even though we'd called her just as we got on the bus like we promised. Then she said, "So, how did everything go today?"

Of course we were prepared. All day, every time we called, we told her a fake story about where we were. So now we just had to remember what we'd said. We'd studied our guidebooks so we could make it all seem more real.

We—actually, mostly Lucas, because she lies to Mom a lot better than I do—told her about our tour of Kensington Palace and not seeing anybody from the royal family, and about what we saw at the two famous stamp shops, and by the time we got done with that, Robert came out from his bedroom dressed for work, asked if we'd had fun, made a few jokes, and headed off for the restaurant. When he left, Mom got right back to work on her article, Lucas and I watched TV for the rest of the night and ate bread and cheese and something called a meat pie that Robert had bought for us to munch on, and we didn't have to answer any more questions.

I was glad. I had the feeling that the more we lied, the more trouble we might get into eventually.

That night when we were packing up our disguises for the next day, I noticed Lucas was quieter than usual.

"What's wrong?" I asked.

She folded up a shirt, stuffed it in a bag, and shrugged. I personally hate it when you're trying to get somebody to say something and all they do is shrug.

I was getting ready to let her have it when she said, "Are you sure we're not doing something totally stupid?"

"Lucas, this was your idea!"

"Well, maybe it was a really crummy idea."

I remembered how excited we were when we'd given each other Oscars in front of the mirror in the women's loo, and I figured I knew what Lucas was feeling.

"I think it's just the letdown," I said, wrapping up a pair of shoes in a plastic bag before putting them in with the other clothes. "It's like after that time we called Brendon Thorpe and I was so excited for a while, and then later I was sure everything we said to him was so stupid." Brendon Thorpe is this cute guy who was in my English class last year. "Remember? I think it always works that way. After you have a big, like, rush or whatever, like talking to Brendon or what we did this afternoon, you're always going to feel let down."

"Maybe. But we have absolutely no real reason to be doing what we're doing. I mean, yeah, it would make sense to make a copy of what Gallery Guy is painting to use as evidence if we ever find out there's been an art crime. But how do we know he's not just some incredibly rude amateur painter who likes to copy paintings by Rembrandt?"

I sat down on the bed and faced her. "Look, Lucas. I know all we have to go on is circumstantial evidence. We don't have any smoking gun."

"Circumstantial evidence? Smoking gun? Girl, you've been watching too many cop shows."

"You know what I mean," I said. "We don't have any real proof that Gallery Guy is doing something illegal, but it sure looks like he is. It's not like we've only seen him in London. Remember, he was in Minneapolis, too, also copying a picture by Rembrandt."

"So maybe he has a lot of money, likes to travel, likes to paint, *plus* likes to copy paintings by Rembrandt."

"Don't tell me he's been working on drawing fingernails for an entire year!" It seemed like she was just being stubborn. "Listen, Lucas, we have a ton of reasons to be suspicious. First, he's been in two different museums, thousands of miles apart, copying pictures by Rembrandt. Second, he's wearing a disguise that makes him look totally different from the guy we saw in Minneapolis. The only reason I can think of for somebody to do that is to make sure nobody who saw him *there* would recognize him *here*.

"Third"—by this time I was holding up my fingers and counting off the points—"the way he leans over his canvas, he for sure doesn't want anybody to see what he's working on. And fourth, both in Minneapolis and here, when somebody tried to see what he's painting, he got all bent out of shape and said, 'Go a-*way*.' Any one of those things could be totally random, but together, you've got to admit, it's suspicious. He must be up to something."

I could tell by Lucas's expression that I was convincing her. "Besides, *as you pointed out*," I added, "if we weren't doing this, what else would we be doing?"

"Yeah, I guess you're right."

There was another argument, but I wasn't going to use it. The thing is, like I've said, Lucas is a lot smarter than I am. I get good grades, but those tests you take in school show that she's almost a genius.

But also like I've said, I have way better intuition than she has. She might get straight As without having to study, and she might get first prize in physics contests, but lots of times I know things without knowing why or how I know them. Not school stuff of course, but about situations, and especially about people and what they're like.

Now my intuition was saying that Gallery Guy was up to something big. And we had to get that painting copied, I just knew it. It seemed like a race against time.

I wasn't going to tell Lucas that. I figured she'd make fun of me if I told her I thought it was a race against time. But I knew we had to do what we were doing, and I knew we had to do it in a hurry, even if I didn't know why.

# The Trouble with Intuition

The next day, Lucas was back to normal. And Mom was finally getting used to us being on our own—she seemed to take our trip into central London for granted.

We had a lot to do that morning, so we got up early. Right after breakfast we grabbed the stuff we'd packed the night before and made one more trip from Robert's place to downtown.

We'd just left the tube station and were crossing an incredibly busy street with about a thousand other pedestrians when Lucas poked me in the side with her elbow and said, "Don't look now, but there's Gallery Guy."

Of course I did look, and there he was, behind the wheel of a long, low, shiny black car that was stopped first in line at the crosswalk. Fortunately he wasn't paying any attention to the people who were walking in a bunch right in front of him.

"Wouldn't you know he'd be driving a Jaguar," Lucas said. "It's so perfect."

I'm not as into cars as she is. "Is that a Jaguar?" I asked. By this time we'd gotten to the other side of the street. I turned around in time to see Gallery Guy's car speed off.

"Haven't you ever seen one before? Some of my parents' friends have them. It's expensive, like a Mercedes or Lexus. The coolest thing is the hood ornament. It's a jaguar springing forward."

"Oh, I've seen those. Why do you think it's like Gallery Guy to have one?"

"I've never known a woman who drives a Jaguar," Lucas explained. "It seems like all the people who own them are guys who want to feel macho and important."

"Yeah, that seems like the kind of person Gallery Guy is, all right."

Before heading into the National Gallery, we had three stops to make. First, we found an ATM and Lucas took out a bunch of money. (Lucas's parents let her have her own ATM card—in some ways it actually does pay to be rich.) Then we found a drugstore where we got some air freshener for the bathroom and a pair of glasses with clear lenses that I could use for a disguise. Finally we stopped at the gift shop at the National Gallery to get an acrylic paint set and a reproduction of *Belshazzar's Feast*.

We'd come up with a plan that would use both Lucas's photographic memory and drawing talent and my talent for painting. Lucas would keep going into the Rembrandt room and do whatever she could to get a good look at what Gallery Guy was painting so she could sketch it all out on our canvas. She'd also draw him sitting at his easel, the way we'd planned.

My part was to get ready to do the painting by studying the way Rembrandt had painted those hands. And that meant I had to go into the Rembrandt room, too.

If I hadn't taken those classes at the Minneapolis Institute of Arts, I would have wondered why Gallery Guy would take a risk like sitting in a busy room in a famous museum to copy Rembrandt's painting instead of just using a copy he could imitate in private.

But those art classes answered that question for me. When the teacher sent us into the galleries to copy paintings, I learned that there's no way to imitate a painter's brushstrokes by working from even a really good copy of a painting. You have to see how thick the paint is and whether it's put on smooth or bumpy, plus the colors on a reproduction are never quite right. That meant even though we'd gotten our own big copy of *Belshazzar's Feast* to use as a guide, I still needed to see the original up close. Because if Gallery Guy was trying to paint the way Rembrandt painted, then I should be trying to paint that way, too.

We went on a few tours. A couple of times we tagged along with families, trying to blend in. Of course every time we went through we used different clothes and hairdos and sometimes used glasses, makeup, or our retainers for even more of a disguise. When one of us left the gallery, we came straight back to the loo to report to each other, change our clothes, and waste a little time before we went in again.

It wasn't so bad for me. Lucas had made a drawing for me of the woman's hands that seemed kind of stuck together, and of the hand that was sticking out of the cloud—at least that one had fingernails—and I was making progress figuring out exactly what brushstrokes and color mixtures Rembrandt used to paint them. I'd work on a section like a shadow or a knuckle while I waited for Lucas.

But after a few trips Lucas started getting frustrated. No matter how hard she tried, she was never able to see very much of the painting.

The way Gallery Guy painted was really weird. He didn't hold a palette in one hand and his brush in the other and stand or sit back from the canvas, like my dad and other painters do. Instead, he had his palette on a little shelf connected to the easel. He was left-handed, and it was on the left side where he could reach with his brush without leaning back. He kept his right arm resting on top of the canvas. He always looked around to make sure nobody was watching him before he left his canvas uncovered to change brushes or reach for a new tube of paint.

It sounds suspicious-looking, but he must have been painting like that for a long time, because he made the way he sat look natural.

Lucas tried everything she could think of to see what was on the middle of the canvas, but she only managed to see the edges. On one trip she spotted the fingertip I'd seen, and actually saw the very top of a second fingertip, but that didn't do us a lot of good. She tried tricks—tying her shoe to see the bottom right corner, dropping her museum map to see the bottom left, but all she saw was a little more of the lacy fabric and the red background.

By this time she wasn't just frustrated, she was *extremely* frustrated.

Instead of drawing what Gallery Guy was painting, she was stuck spending all her time in the bathroom making sketches of him on a big art tablet we'd bought in the museum shop. She drew him from a bunch of angles, then did an awesome drawing of him with the Rembrandt paintings around him. You could even tell which paintings were which from what she drew.

One thing about Lucas, she isn't a quitter. She kept on trying. But as the afternoon went on, I started having a little feeling that we should quit. Pack up and go home.

It was my intuition talking to me. But did I pay attention? NoooOOOoooo.

See, I wanted to get one more look at Rembrandt's

brushstrokes on the woman's middle finger. So I decided to go in again. I put on a long, baggy white shirt, a pair of khakis and my Sketchers, pulled my hair back in a ponytail, and walked to Gallery 22, waiting for something to happen. Sure enough, along came a guided tour in Spanish, and I tagged along behind. The guide stopped in front of Rembrandt's self-portrait, and I'd just turned toward Gallery Guy's canvas when, miracle of miracles, he actually leaned over to get a new brush out of his metal kit on the floor *without glancing around first to see if anyone was looking.*

In all the time we'd watched him, he'd never done anything so careless before. He only moved about a foot before he caught himself and straightened back up, but I'd seen what was in the middle of his painting.

It was a huge set of hands coming out of gold sleeves. The fingers were twined together, the palms resting on a rounded something painted cream and gold. The painting was so beautiful I almost gasped. Before Gallery Guy could look around to see if I was looking—which I knew he would—I quick turned in the other direction.

And I looked straight at Bert, who was looking straight at me. I mean *straight* at me. Glaring.

My heart started beating like the drum at the end of a heavy metal song. I froze. What should I do. Stay? Run? What?

But then I could almost hear Lucas saying, "Stay cool,

Kari." So I pretended like nothing had happened. I walked with the Spanish group into the next room, then kept walking as fast as I could without looking suspicious through the room that led from there to the education wing and down the stairs to the women's loo.

"I've got some good news and some bad news," I said, bursting through the door, and I told Lucas what had happened.

She listened, then leaned against the counter with the sinks in it, folded her arms across her chest, and stared up toward the ceiling.

Finally she said, "You'd better cool it for a while. Bert strikes me as the 'stick your nose in everybody else's business' type who might feel it was his duty or something to tell Gallery Guy he's being spied on."

That was fine with me. I didn't *want* to go back. "Okay, from now on it's up to you."

She turned around and used the mirror to look at me. "I'm getting sick of this. I've made six trips trying to see the middle of his canvas. I think it's time I just make it happen."

She straightened and moved toward the door. "I'm going to make one last trip through since I'm already dressed for it, and this time I'm going to be aggressive. What have we got to lose?" With that she was out of the loo before I could say anything back.

I settled on the floor next to the sink, the canvas in my

lap and the paints beside me, and thought about what she'd just said. What *did* we have to lose? If she once got a good look at the canvas, we didn't need to see Gallery Guy ever again. Or Bert either, for that matter.

But somehow I still didn't want Gallery Guy to know what we were up to. He was a bad guy, and there was no telling what he'd do if he knew he was being spied on.

Ten minutes later, Lucas walked back into the restroom, cool as could be, and announced, "I just had a fight with Gallery Guy."

# Snakes, a Sari, and Nerves of Steel

"You *what?*" I stood up so fast I almost dropped the canvas.

"Gallery Guy caught me. I think Bert might have talked to him after he saw you and told him he was being spied on. Anyway, I was doing the tagging-along-with-a-family routine and I got closer to his canvas than usual, like I said I would, when he flung this cloth over it, got off his stool, and said, 'Why are you spying on me?'"

My eyes felt like they'd pop out of my face. "What did you say?" I almost shouted.

"I said, 'That question seems to mean you have something to hide.'"

Only Lucas could have come up with that answer. She's going to make a heck of a lawyer.

She'd worn her hair up on this trip, and now she started undoing it. "'I saw you here spying on me yesterday, too,' he said, and I said, 'So?' Then I crossed my arms and waited for him to talk. One of my dad's favorite sayings is, 'Whoever speaks first, loses.'"

By this time she was brushing out her hair. "So then he said, 'Get out. I don't want to see you here again.' And I said, 'You must be kidding. Who's going to stop me?'"

"And what did *he* say?" My chest felt heavy just thinking about it.

"He said, '*I* will, and it would be better for you if you don't have to find out how.' He does have an accent, by the way."

"And you said . . ."

"I said, 'Up yours, meep.'" Believe me, meep wasn't the word she said. "Then I left."

I took a great huge breath. "Didn't you die of fright?"

She looked at me, totally calm. "Do I look dead?"

"But how could you say those things?"

"Grandma Stickney always says the best way to deal with a bully is to bully him back."

She looked like she'd just told me that she'd walked to the grocery store to buy a quart of milk.

"Let's get out of here." I started washing paintbrushes.

"We're not giving up, you know," Lucas said. "I'm going to get a look at that canvas one way or another."

"You're not actually thinking about coming back here after what just happened!"

"Wanna bet?"

"But Lucas, he's seen you! This guy's dangerous! This started out being fun, but now it's beginning to feel really scary. Getting a copy of that canvas isn't worth it!"

"What if we did it in a way that made *absolutely sure* he wouldn't recognize us?"

"How? We've already used our disguises. Lucas, this guy is a snake!"

She looked at my reflection in the mirror for a minute, then she got a sneaky little smile on her face. "Two can play at that game."

That evening we were eating dinner at Robert's restaurant with Mom and Celia again, when Mom turned to Lucas and me and said, "I'd like you guys to help me tomorrow."

I almost choked on my burger.

"I'm meeting the photographer for the "London Looks" shoot tomorrow morning and it would be great to have you there," she continued. "There's always so much stuff to keep track of. You'd be a big help."

Lucas and I looked at each other. We both gulped.

"What's the problem?" Mom asked.

"Well"—I thought as fast as I could—"I want to take Lucas to see the costumes you did that article on, the ones in the Victoria and Albert Museum."

"And we kind of thought we could spend most of our

day tomorrow in that part of town," Lucas said. "We've been talking about it a lot."

"Yeah, and we still have some pictures to take in costumes, for Lucas's mom," I added. "Of course, if you really need us to help . . ."

"Well, we're doing another shoot on Saturday. If you absolutely promise to help me then, no argument."

Of course we said we would. We just needed one more day to finish up at the National Gallery, and we wanted to make sure that day came before Gallery Guy finished what he was doing and cleared out.

I felt bad about not helping Mom when she needed us. Plus I didn't like this lying. She does have a suspicious mind, and she is intuitive, so I kept worrying she'd know we weren't telling the truth. But it wasn't just that that made me uncomfortable.

The rules about lying are pretty complicated. First, you're taught that lying is wrong. Then when you're about eight or so, you start learning about the kind of lying that's okay. The kind you do not to hurt people's feelings, like telling your relatives you like the Christmas gifts they gave you even if you don't. But this lying to Mom was in the first category. I knew it wasn't right, and I felt guilty for doing something that was so obviously wrong. Besides, I had the feeling that eventually I was going to have to pay for doing it. Big-time.

I was still thinking about this when I heard Lucas say, "Celia, where would I go to buy a black wig?"

Both Mom and Celia looked at her, startled.

"Why would you need a black wig?" Mom asked.

"To go with my sari," Lucas said. We'd already told Celia about all our clothes, and having to take pictures. The saris were still in our suitcases, about the only things we hadn't worn. "I should probably not be wearing a sari at all since I'm not from India or Pakistan, but what makes it even worse is that I'm a blonde," Lucas said. "Besides, I thought it would be fun to freak my mom out a little bit."

"I feel like a coconspirator," Celia said, smiling and rubbing her hands together. "I have a black wig. I used to use it for auditions when I was trying out for Latin parts. And how about some dark makeup?"

After she and Celia finished discussing the disguise, Lucas said, "Oh, and Gillian, do you remember when you said I could use the leather jacket whenever I wanted to and you could borrow Celia's raincoat?"

"Mm-hmm," Mom answered. "Want to use it tomorrow?"

"Yeah, if it's not too much trouble."

"Well I should think you could, since it's actually yours."

"No it isn't. It's yours now," Lucas said, "but I think tomorrow's a good day to take that picture with me wearing it."

The next day we took the leather jacket, one sari, the wig, and the makeup to the city center, stopped at the drugstore again, found a pet shop, and entered the museum, ready to go to war with a snake.

About one thirty in the afternoon, Lucas walked into the Rembrandt room. She was wearing the turquoise sari draped over her head and she carried the end of the fabric over one arm. She was all done up in Celia's wig, she had a red dot on her forehead, kohl pencil around her eyes, and wherever you could see her skin we'd put dark makeup on it. Except for her blue eyes, she looked just like the girls from India and Pakistan who are always wandering around Trafalgar Square.

If you looked closely, you could see that under where the sari hung over her arm she was carrying a little box.

Coming into the room about thirty seconds after her, wearing torn jeans and a dirty T-shirt, a leather jacket, a ring through her eyebrow (fake), a row of pierced earrings in her left ear (fake), one big metal stud in her right ear (real), and spiked-out hair, was yours truly, feeling excited, terrified, and stupid, all at the same time.

We were following a bunch of French tourists on a guided tour.

Lucas turned in the opposite direction from Gallery Guy and *Belshazzar's Feast* as soon as she came in the door. I went over to hang around the edge of the French tour group. They were all standing on one side of Gallery Guy, looking at Rembrandt's self-portrait. I stood just on the other side.

Lucas sauntered around as if looking at the paintings, moving closer and closer to where Gallery Guy was sitting and I was standing. She seemed to drop something on the floor, and leaned over as if to pick it up. Then she casually stepped over in my direction.

Suddenly somebody yelled something in French, and all meep broke loose. People were running and pushing, women were screaming and men were shouting.

And the word all the French people were using was something that sounded like *"Sair-pah, sair-pah!"*

It was French for serpent. Because there was an eighteen-inch snake crawling across the middle of the floor.

The place was totally panicked. Bert must have pulled a switch, because the museum alarms went off. Guards poured in from both entrances.

The doors were blocked with French people trying to get out, and other people trying to get in to see what the fuss was about. People kept screaming. One of the guards yelled, "Stay calm, stay calm." The French guide was yelling something that sounded like *"Calm-may voo! Calm-may voo!"* A couple of the guards were walking around the room, making sure all the paintings were safe and talking into little walkie-talkies.

Bert was running around after the snake. Another guard said, "Pick up the bleedin' thing!"

"I hate ruddy snakes!" Bert yelled back.

Obviously Gallery Guy didn't like snakes either. Lucas

had let the creature out of its box right behind him, then she'd given it a poke with her toe so it would go right toward the easel. Seeing it curve across the floor almost at his feet, Gallery Guy jumped from his stool. I was standing so close that when he popped up he almost knocked me over.

That's what was supposed to happen. Now it was time for my big part. "Watchit, Dad," I said in my best East Ender accent, just like Robert had taught me, and I gave Gallery Guy a shove with my elbow, which made him stumble and knock over his easel.

While he was trying to get his balance and watching so he didn't step on the snake, Gallery Guy was too distracted to notice Lucas, who was busy memorizing the lines and colors of the big set of hands in the middle of his canvas, now lying on the floor in plain sight.

It wasn't until Bert marched from the room, grasping the wriggling snake by what you might call the neck if snakes had necks and holding it way out in front of him, that Gallery Guy remembered his canvas, and by that time Lucas had seen what she needed to see and was flouncing out of the room, where I was waiting for her.

I tell you, that girl has nerves of steel.

## What Happened to Bert

All the way back to Robert's we were totally pumped. We'd planned it so we'd get back earlier than anyone else that afternoon. We ended up with almost an hour and a half to work on drawing the hands. Lucas was close to finished when somebody came in, and we slid our painting and drawing things under a bed upstairs in the loft that was our bedroom.

On Saturday we helped Mom do "London Looks," this time at Covent Garden, where Lucas and I spent most of our time watching the buskers, or street entertainers. That night Robert had to work, and Mom and Celia went out to have a fancy dinner and hear some jazz. The minute everyone was gone, we pulled our canvas out again and spent six whole hours painting the hands as well as Lucas could remember them, with me trying to make the brushstrokes and color mixtures look like Rembrandt's. Lucas thought I did a great job. I'd spent enough time studying Rembrandt's paintings to know that it wasn't great, but it was the best I could do in a hurry.

When the canvas was dry, we rolled it up with the drawings Lucas had made of Gallery Guy on her sketch pad and the print we'd bought of *Belshazzar's Feast*, and stuck the whole roll in the cardboard poster tube the print came in. We figured we could take it back home that way and Mom would just think it was the print.

Then we put our paints and dirty brushes in a plastic shopping bag and dropped the whole thing into the garbage can (what Robert calls the dustbin) out by his garden shed and opened Robert's windows to make sure we got rid of the paint smell.

And that was that. It made me depressed. It was like we were saying good-bye to our whole adventure in London, and absolutely nothing had come of it. I wished we could just go home and I could forget about the whole thing. Instead, we were stuck there for three more days.

What I didn't know was that some of the most important parts of our London adventure were still to come.

On Sunday we took a drive in the English countryside. But on Monday it was pouring down rain and the forecast said it would probably rain all day. The last thing Mom had to do before we left on Wednesday was another "London

Looks," which she wanted to do outdoors if possible, so she decided to take the day off.

It was Mom's choice about what to do, because she hadn't had any time to sightsee. Guess where she wanted to go.

The National Gallery.

"Great," Lucas said when she and I went back up to our loft. "We get to go back and see all those paintings we've seen a billion times."

"We could give her our own guided tour," I said.

"I could even give her a guided tour in French," Lucas responded, with a dry look.

"Maybe we can go back to the women's loo in the education section, just for old time's sake."

"Spray a little air freshener." That one got me giggling.

"You know, this won't be the first time we've gone through the National Gallery with a grown-up. But it *will* be the first time we've gone with a grown-up who's ever laid eyes on us before," I said, and now Lucas was giggling, too.

"I might have to fight an uncontrollable urge to run into the restroom and change my clothes," she added.

By this time we were laughing hysterically. After we'd gotten control of ourselves, I said, "I bet Gallery Guy's gone. He was almost finished with what he was doing, and I bet he's left town."

"We'll have to at least sneak a peek."

For a second I thought about telling Lucas I didn't want to even go back and *peek* into the Rembrandt room. But then I realized that even if Gallery Guy was still there and saw us and recognized Lucas, there was nothing he could really do to us in the middle of a museum, especially with Mom there. I have to admit, having her around made me feel safer.

Mom is way more serious about looking at art than we are, and besides, she knew we'd already visited the museum. So we told her we wanted to go around on our own, and we'd meet her later in the cafeteria. As soon as we made sure she'd started on a whole other part of the museum, we wandered away to the Rembrandt room.

We took the roundabout way and ended up in Gallery 24, where we'd waited out of Bert's sight on our first day spying on Gallery Guy. Standing back and looking through the doorway, we weren't surprised to see Gallery Guy's usual spot empty. That was a relief.

"Well, we don't have to hide anymore," Lucas said, and walked through the Rembrandt room toward the door to Gallery 22. And surprise surprise, somebody besides Bert was standing guard.

"Wonder what's up with Bert today," Lucas muttered.

"Maybe he has a cold or something."

"Or maybe they moved him to another gallery. Let's

ask," she said, and before I could comment, she'd walked straight up to the new guard.

"How can I help you?" the guard said. He was short and wiry, with red cheeks and bright blue eyes, and he had a really big accent.

"We were wondering about Bert, the guard who's usually here. Is he absent today?" Lucas asked.

The guard suddenly looked very serious. "How did you know old Bert? He wasn't your uncle or nothing, was he?"

"No, we don't know him," Lucas said. "We just saw him in here sometimes, that's all."

"I have bad news for you, missies," the guard said slowly. "Bert died Saturday, on his way home from his half-day shift. Got run over by a bus, he did."

"Saturday!" I said. "But we just saw him on Friday." I felt like somebody had punched me. And from the look on Lucas's face, I think she felt the same.

"That's how these things go, my dears. Terrible shock, it was. He lived alone, did old Bert, so at least he didn't leave behind no missus or little kiddies needin' a dad."

"But how did it happen?" Lucas asked. "Did he just fall, or what?"

"We-e-e-ll," the guard began, and the way he said it, you knew he was winding up to tell us something interesting, "there's a woman was behind him in the queue, says he was pushed."

Then, seeing our horrified expressions, he continued, "Oh yes, she says she saw a man push him under the on-coming bus. But others say it was an accident, and that's what I think, too. I don't know why anybody would want to push old Bert. He was harmless enough.

"It's been quite a week around here, with Bert's accident coming right after the snake incident and all."

"What snake incident?" I said. I knew perfectly well what snake incident.

"We-e-e-ll," he wound himself up again, "it was last Friday, it was. About the middle of the afternoon. Suddenly this here snake starts roamin' the galleries. Old Henry, he was the first one as seen it, over in the Impressionist section. Ted says he thought he seen somethin' out of the corner of his eye. That's in Eye-talian Ren-AY-zance." He meant *Italian Renaissance*.

Lucas and I looked at each other. We knew that snake had only been on the floor for approximately ninety seconds, and only in the Rembrandt room.

"Then it crawled in here. Caused quite a stir, it did. Old Bert, he picked it up and carried it out, brave as you please, though he said afterward it near gave him heart failure. Well, it would, wouldn't it? Everyone bein' so afraid of snakes and all."

We didn't tell him that we weren't the slightest bit afraid of snakes.

"The incident even made it into the *Mirror*."

"What?" Lucas was almost shouting. The *Daily Mirror* is a newspaper.

"Not as you'd say a big article. Still, Bert got his name in it. Hope it made his last day a little happier, poor bloke.

"I says to my missus, I says, 'It's eerie, him dying like that after just handling a snake. It's as if that snake was a omen, like.'"

I don't know when I've felt quite as miserable as I did after hearing about Bert dying. For one thing, just to know that someone you'd seen alive almost the day before was now dead was weird, and it made me sad, even though I didn't much like Bert when he was alive.

But there was something else, something totally huge that made me feel like I'd been socked in the stomach. With everything that was going on with Gallery Guy, I didn't think Bert's death was just an accident. Somebody had pushed him under that bus. And I kept thinking about those last words of the guard, the ones about the snake being an omen. Was there any connection between the snake incident and what happened to Bert? Because if there was, then in some way Lucas and I were responsible for his death.

# The Jaguar

Tuesday was a beautiful, sunny day. Not the kind of day when you expect something terrible to happen.

We were helping Mom with "London Looks" in a little park called Sloane Square in a busy part of town where there are lots of clothes shops and fashionable people. When we weren't doing something for Mom, we sat in the sunshine, writing in our travel journals. I hadn't written much since the whole thing with Gallery Guy had started the week before, so getting it all down, including my feelings about Bert dying, was going to take hours.

Lucas never seems to write as much as I do, and after about the first half hour I noticed that she was drawing on the journal pages. She did more sketches of Gallery Guy, and a big drawing of the hands with the intertwined fingers in the middle of Gallery Guy's canvas.

A little after noon, Mom gave us some money and asked us to walk a few blocks down a big street called King's Road to this little sandwich-and-salad takeout place called Pret a Manger to get us all some lunch.

The last thing Mom said before we left was, "It's busy around here, so be extra careful of the traffic."

Lucas and I looked at each other and rolled our eyes. We'd been walking around London for days in places a lot busier than Sloane Square and nothing had happened yet. We'd gotten good at it.

We found the place, no problem, and got our food.

"I'm hungry," I said when we were back outside and I was stuffing the drinks on top of the hoodie in Lucas's backpack.

"Me, too. Let's get going."

We took off at a trot. There was traffic up and down King's Road, but not anywhere near as bad as around Trafalgar Square.

Halfway down the first block a little kid got loose from his mom and ran straight into my legs. By the time his mother got hold of him again, Lucas was way ahead of me, just about to cross a quiet side street with no traffic lights.

She was running the last few steps to the corner when I noticed the car coming up beside me on King's Road—driving on the left-hand side of the road, of course, like they do in London. It was black and long and low and shiny. It wasn't slowing down and didn't have its blinker on. It was just another car in London traffic.

Then, at the very last minute, it speeded up and was suddenly turning left into the street Lucas was just going to cross.

I saw her, still trotting, turn her head the other way, to make sure no one was coming on the side street, then step off the curb and onto the pavement.

The car revved its engine as it roared around the corner, tires squealing. One more second—maybe half a second, maybe less—and the little silver jaguar on the hood of the car would be aimed directly at Lucas.

"LUUUCAAAS!" I screamed from way down in my throat, the loudest I've ever screamed in my life. I was sure I was too late. I was sure she'd be smashed, thrown to the pavement, run over.

She heard me just in time. Her head snapped to the right. She saw the car. I know this can't be true—she must have touched ground somewhere in there—but it seemed like she actually stopped and reversed in midair. I watched as she flew backward, saw the heel of her shoe hit the curb as she went down, falling, falling—but onto the sidewalk, not into the street.

She landed hard smack on her butt. Beyond her the black car sped away, tires still squealing.

Then it was quiet, and Lucas was sitting there. Somehow her backpack had slipped off her shoulders, the straps now around her elbows, and she was sitting on it.

I dropped to my knees next to her. "Are you okay?"

She grunted.

A youngish guy with supershort hair ran toward us from across the little street.

"Are you hurt?" he asked.

"No," Lucas said. "At least I don't think so."

"Any painful bits?" he asked.

"Just . . . the part I sit on."

He held out his hand and helped Lucas struggle to her feet. She took a few wobbly steps.

"Would have been worse without the rucksack," the guy said. I figured that must be the British word for *backpack*.

I looked down. Lucas had landed on the hoodie, but she must have gotten a couple of the plastic bottles, too. I could see orange juice oozing out from one side onto the sidewalk.

"Driver must have been a nutter," the guy said, "speeding around the corner like that. Miracle he didn't hit you."

"Did you see what he looked like?" I asked.

"Nah, can't say I noticed. Just some toff in a Jaguar." He pronounced it like *jag-you-are*.

He turned to Lucas. "So you're all right then? Nothing broken? You're sure now?"

Lucas held up a hand, which was badly skinned at the

bottom of the palm, then flexed her wrist. "Yeah, I'm sure. Thank you."

"Right." The guy hesitated. "Well, I'll be off then."

He gave Lucas a last, uncertain look.

"Right," he said again. "Cheers." Then away he went.

"You want to sit down?" I asked.

"Yeah. I guess so," Lucas muttered. I pointed behind her, toward a bench a few steps from the corner. I grabbed her leaking backpack and helped her over.

She sucked in her breath and let out a little moan as she sat down. "I'm going to have some heavy-duty black and blue marks. Kari—"

"Yes?"

"Kari, thank you for screaming at me like that. If you hadn't, I'd probably have been run over."

"No big deal. Anybody would have done it."

"It *is* a big deal, Kari. You saved my life. That guy we just talked to was right. The driver must have been nuts."

"Um, Lucas—"

I was just about to say something about the driver of the Jaguar, when I saw Mom coming down the sidewalk. When she got to us she said, "I looked over and saw you limping. What's up?"

"Lucas had an almost-but-not-quite accident," I said.

"No! Are you hurt?" Mom dropped to her knees in front of Lucas, her expression suddenly serious.

"Not really. My butt's going to be black and blue, is all."

"What happened?" Mom asked. She looked alarmed, and her eyebrows were pulled almost completely together.

"It was my fault," Lucas said. "It was the first time since we got here that I forgot about the driving-on-the-left thing. I didn't look behind me to see if anybody was coming up in the left lane wanting to turn in front of me."

"That's not how it happened!" I said. "You didn't see the whole thing. I did. It wouldn't have mattered if you'd have looked, Lucas. The guy didn't have his blinker on or anything, and at the last minute he just squealed around the corner without any warning."

"When Kari saw the car turn she screamed, or I would have been hit."

"Crazy driver! He should go to jail!" Mom was almost shouting, she was so upset. "Did you fall? What happened?"

"I ended up sitting down smack on my backpack on the sidewalk."

I held up the dripping backpack to show Mom.

"You're sure you didn't injure anything?"

"Like I told you, my butt hurts. That's all. And I skinned my hand." She held up her scratched palm.

"You're white as a sheet, and you're shaking." Mom was up close now, looking into Lucas's face.

"Yeah, I guess I am a little." I couldn't believe it. I'd never seen her get shaky about anything. Nobody asked me how I was feeling, and I didn't want to say anything since I wasn't the one who was hurt, but to be honest, I was shaky, too.

Mom got to her feet and helped Lucas up just like the guy had done. "Kari, why don't you run up and tell the photographer to be back in an hour? Let's find a restaurant and have a nice, relaxing lunch. And you need some strong tea with lots of sugar, young lady," she said to Lucas. "It's what the English would prescribe, and it's probably as good for you as anything."

After she ate, Lucas seemed better and her face was a lot less pale. I had some tea, too, and I was feeling more normal. Lucas said she didn't want to go back to Robert's, so we stopped at a store and got a couple cushions for her to sit on, then went back to our park bench.

And that was the first chance I had to talk to Lucas about what I was thinking. I let her get all comfortable and waited until Mom and the photographer were busy, then I said, "Uh, Lucas. About that car that almost hit you."

"What about it?"

"Remember that day when we saw Gallery Guy in his car outside Charing Cross station?"

"Of course. In his Jaguar." Then she looked at me, and it was obvious she knew what I was going to say. "Don't even go there, Kari. It was not Gallery Guy driving that car."

"How do you know?"

"Because it doesn't make sense. He couldn't have

known where we'd be today. Even your mom didn't know until she and the photographer decided."

"I don't think Gallery Guy was *stalking* us," I said. "I think he just happened to be driving along King's Road, saw you, and decided in a split second to try to take you out."

"Take me out! You're always talking like a TV cop."

"Kill you. Whatever." I was beginning to lose my temper. A couple hours before, I'd saved her life. Now she was mocking me. I counted to ten, like Mom always tells me to do when I get mad, then said, "I think Gallery Guy will kill anybody who sees what he's doing."

"You think he just *happened* to be driving on King's Road, and *happened* to see me, as I *happened* to be crossing a street? You'd have to be stupid to believe in that many coincidences."

When Lucas starts talking to me like that, I want to hit her. Since I'm not into violence, the next best thing is to say as little to her as possible until we've had some time apart. Thank goodness this was our last day in London.

# An Orphan at 30,000 Feet

Flying across the ocean takes a long time, and the day we flew back from London it seemed like I had 283 hours to think. What I was thinking was that I was partly responsible for Bert's murder. And even though I was sitting for nine hours in an airplane between my mother and my so-called best friend, I couldn't talk to anybody about it.

I sure wasn't going to talk to Lucas. I was still so mad at her I probably had steam coming out of my ears. Even if she was right about Gallery Guy not being the driver of the Jaguar, she didn't have to be so snotty about it. Especially right after I'd saved her life. Yeah, it did seem like a lot of coincidences that Lucas would be crossing a street just when Gallery Guy came driving along and could run her down, but coincidences do happen.

If she was miserable sitting on her butt all those hours,

it about served her right. Getting back to Minnesota and dropping her off at her house was the one thought that made me happy.

So that took care of Lucas. Trouble was, I couldn't talk to my mom about the Bert thing and how guilty I felt about it either. And I sure couldn't tell her what I suspected about the Jaguar. I don't want to sound like I'm still a little kid or anything, but when I have a really big problem, Mom's always been the person I wanted to talk to. Well, remember what I said about knowing I was going to have to pay big-time for telling all those lies? I thought eventually I'd be grounded or lose my allowance or not be able to use the phone or the Internet or something.

But instead, at least so far, it looked like my punishment was going to be not being able to talk to my mom when I really needed to. What could I tell her? That everything we'd said to her in London had been lies, all lies? To say we did it for a good cause—well, that might mean something to me, but when it came to my mom I didn't think it would cut it.

The only answer was to keep my mouth shut. So there I sat with one part of me feeling like a terrible, no-good murderer, one part still wondering if Gallery Guy had almost killed Lucas, and still another part feeling like an orphan. As punishment went, believe me, this was way worse than losing telephone and IM privileges.

I was so tired because of everything that had happened

and the after-excitement letdown that about halfway over the Atlantic Ocean I got all teary-eyed feeling guilty and alone. Just then the flight attendant came by and I got some orange juice and drank it, and I felt a little better.

When I was done I pulled out my journal and did a little summary of the Gallery Guy mystery. I knew Mom wouldn't look at what I was writing because she doesn't believe in reading other people's journals. I wrote:

## WHERE WE ARE WITH
## THE GALLERY GUY MYSTERY

*Things we're almost absolutely sure about:*

1. The guy painting in the National Gallery is the same one who was painting in the Minneapolis Art Institute.

2. He's planning an art crime of some sort. Theory: It has to do with forging a painting by Rembrandt.

3. He's practicing some hands he's going to have in his own picture.

4. He's using disguises so that people like Lucas and me who see him in both places won't recognize him.

5. If there is a crime, and if we hear about it, our canvas and Lucas's drawings of Gallery Guy in the Rembrandt gallery will be a big clue.

*Questions:*

1. Who is Gallery Guy, and what exactly is he up to?
2. Has he visited other museums and copied from paintings there?
3. What do the painting of Lucretia in the Art Institute, *Belshazzar's Feast*, and Gallery Guy's painting of hands all have to do with each other?
4. What if some big art crime happens and we don't ever hear about it?
5. What if the crime goes so smoothly for Gallery Guy and his accomplices, if there are any, that nobody ever catches on?
6. If something actually happens and we do hear about it, who will we give our clues to?
7. Why exactly was Bert killed?
8. Is it possible Gallery Guy didn't have anything to do with Bert's death?
9. Did Gallery Guy try to run Lucas down on King's Road?

*Possible reasons why Gallery Guy might have murdered Bert:*

1. Gallery Guy thought Bert saw the canvas when we let out the snake.
2. Gallery Guy thought Bert saw the canvas some other time.

3. Gallery Guy killed him because Bert said something to him about us spying on him.
4. Gallery Guy didn't kill Bert because of anything having to do with us. He killed him because Bert could put two and two together and maybe identify him if any big crime happened involving a painting by Rembrandt.

And then, after writing that much, I added in big letters, AND IF THAT'S TRUE, AND GALLERY GUY HAS COPIED PAINTINGS IN OTHER MUSEUMS, THEN BERT MIGHT NOT BE THE ONLY MUSEUM GUARD GALLERY GUY HAS KILLED!

I was still thinking about what I'd written when Mom, who was in the window seat, asked us to move so she could go to the loo. The idea that Gallery Guy had killed other guards seemed so important that when Mom left, I turned to Lucas and said, "I've thought of something."

"Are we talking animal, vegetable, or mineral here?" she said sarcastically.

"Forget it," I said in my best freeze-out voice. "Just forget it."

These were almost the first two things I'd said to her since she'd called me stupid. I made up my mind they were going to be the last for a very long time.

Uncle Geoff picked us up from the airport. Exactly twenty-three minutes after getting in his car, we dropped Lucas at her house, and two minutes after that we were home.

Geoff had bought some groceries so we wouldn't be coming home to an empty refrigerator. When we got into the house, I played with Guido, the cat we share with Uncle Geoff, and Mom made us some café au lait—with whipped cream and sprinkles for me—brought it out on a tray with some Mint Milano cookies, and put it on the coffee table.

When we'd both had our first bite of cookie, she said, "Okay, what exactly is going on?"

# The Mother Myth

Mothers have a way of finding things out, even when you don't want them to. They seem to have a special intuition about their kids. This means you can't get away with much. The good side is that if you're far away from your mom and something bad happens, chances are the phone will ring and it will be her. Out of the blue.

Uncle Geoff calls it the Mother Myth, the "myth" being that mothers know everything. They don't, but they know plenty.

I should have known we couldn't get away with what we were doing in London.

So when Mom asked me what was going on, I said, of course, "What do you mean?"

And she said, "What do you mean, what do I mean? You know what I mean. In London. What were you and Lucas up to?"

I took a sip of my coffee. "Isn't a mother supposed to say, 'Honey, Sweetie, Daughter That I Love, do you have something you want to tell me about?'"

"Don't push it."

I put my cup down. "Okay, I'll tell you, but my body still thinks we're in London, where it's, like, two in the morning, and I have jet lag. Couldn't we talk about this tomorrow?"

"Nope," she said. "I want you weak and tired and helpless so you can't come up with any tall stories."

Here I was, sort of glad to have a chance to talk with my mother about everything, plus trying to figure out what I was better off covering up, and because of jet lag I felt like every movement my brain was making was in super slow motion.

So I told her—very, very carefully. I started out with the man who'd been copying the painting of Lucretia at the Art Institute, and the "Go a-*way*" thing. And then I told her how we'd seen the same man in London, only disguised, probably doing something that had to do with art forgery.

"How do you know it was the same guy?" she asked.

"It was the way he said 'Go a-*way*.' I'll never forget the way he sounded. That was about the meanest thing anybody ever said to me in my whole life up until then."

"You've lived a very sheltered life," she said dryly.

"Besides, Lucas recognized his face from Minneapolis, even though he was wearing a disguise."

"That photographic memory thing of hers," she muttered.

I told her that we visited the National Gallery every day for the next three days. I didn't tell her that we spent all day every day doing it. I told her about the hands. I told her about a few of the disguises. I told her about our painting and drawing, and I pulled the painting of the hands out of the poster tube and showed it to her. I let her believe we made our copy of the big middle set of hands from what I saw when Gallery Guy reached over to get his paint that time.

"Then," I said, sitting back down and getting to the end of my story, "when we went back to the National Gallery with you, Gallery Guy was gone, which didn't surprise us, but the guard in the Rembrandt room was also gone." I hadn't expected it, but saying this made me want to cry. "And we found out from the other guard that he'd been pushed out in front of a bus."

Now remember, I hadn't had any sleep for something like nineteen hours, and it hadn't exactly been a wonderful day, and all that. I think that was why I started to get tears in my eyes, and I couldn't stop my lip from trembling.

"Oh, honey!" Mom said, and put her arms around me in that embarrassing way parents have. I hadn't planned on breaking into tears, but it happened at just the right time. With Mom fussing over me, I had that many more seconds to figure out what I was going to say next. I was getting to the trickiest part.

"Well, I think it might have been our fault he got killed. I think," I gulped, "I think we might have been partly responsible." No way was I going to tell her about the snake.

I straightened up. I finally had my story ready. "See, when I saw what was in the middle of Gallery Guy's canvas, the guard, his name was Bert, saw me looking, and he might have told Gallery Guy, and if he did, then Gallery Guy might have thought Bert knew too much and . . . and bumped him off."

Mom thought about that for a minute, as if trying to figure out what I'd said. Remember, she had jet lag, too. "No wonder you were looking so miserable on the plane," she said finally. "Kari, I don't want to discount everything you've told me, but you don't know for *sure* that Gallery Guy was doing anything wrong. Face it: it's not likely that you and Lucas would have stumbled onto something like that. So it follows that Bert's death probably has nothing at all to do with Gallery Guy."

Parents should learn that it's exactly this kind of thing that keeps their kids from talking to them in the first place.

I suppose the expression on my face must have shown my feelings, because she said quickly, "Besides, even if it's all true, and even if Gallery Guy *did* push Bert under the bus, you don't know that you had anything to do with it."

"No," I said, blowing my nose. "And I'm not sure that *was* how it happened. Mom, I'm sure that Gallery Guy is up to something illegal. But I've been thinking about how it was a museum guard that died, and it seems like there's a chance that every time Gallery Guy spends a long time in one museum, he kills off anybody who sees him there who might recognize him later." I couldn't help thinking about Lucas on King's Road.

"So what you're saying is, assuming he's doing something fishy, he might have killed a guard at the Art Institute."

I nodded.

I could tell that Mom hadn't quite believed that Gallery Guy was doing anything illegal, and as for the business about him maybe having killed Bert—well, she didn't buy that at all. You know how parents are when you try to tell them something.

But the next day, to keep me from bugging her, she called somebody she knew who'd worked at the Art Institute for a long time. Yes, Mom's friend said, she remembered that a little over a year ago one of the museum guards had died suddenly. It might have been around the time of the *Lucretia* exhibit. How did he die? Oh, he was killed by a hit-and-run driver.

At the end of the call Mom just stood there for a second looking at the phone, then she turned to me and said, "Maybe you're on to something."

It was all I could do not to tell her about the Jaguar.

As for my punishment, it was pretty bad. I was grounded and lost phone and Internet privileges for three whole weeks (which, as it turned out, was almost exactly long enough to stop being mad at Lucas). I also didn't get to buy one single new piece of clothing for the rest of the school year and the entire summer. I got to know the Salvation Army Thrift Store really well. It would have been way worse if I'd told Mom the whole truth, but I never did.

# 22

# Love Lives of the Gleesome Threesome, and Trying to Do the Right Thing

Lucas and I were back to being friends way before school was even out. Except for my joining the Y swim class, Lucas taking tennis lessons, and both of us playing soccer on the same team—oh, and a week with my dad—I don't remember much about the nonmystery part of our lives over the rest of the school year and the first part of summer except what somebody with an incredibly twisted sense of humor might call our love lives.

Lucas had liked this guy named Eric all semester, and finally, at the end of the year, he took her to the spring dance at her school and actually kissed her. More than once. Then, exactly eleven days later, he moved with his family to Austin, Texas. So much for Lucas.

Then there was Mom. She tried Internet dating. She

went out with fourteen guys in six weeks. She said almost all of them were nice, but she didn't want a second date with any of them. After that she gave up looking because it took up too much time.

As for me, a guy in my geography class that I'd been joking around with asked me to a dance, and I turned him down and got flak from absolutely everybody. See, I like him a lot, but only as a friend, and I thought if I went out with him he'd get the wrong idea. Well, Lucas thought he'd tell all the other guys that I didn't accept dates, so nobody would ever ask me out. Mom and some of my school friends thought I should have given the relationship a chance. But all their talking didn't change my mind. I still think I did the right thing.

One good thing about our love lives. Bringing you up to date doesn't take long.

And now we move right from one depressing subject to another: the mystery.

The best thing was that after we found out the Art Institute guard had probably been killed by Gallery Guy, I stopped feeling so guilty about Bert being murdered, even though I still felt bad about him dying. The problem was what to do about the things we were figuring out.

Thanks to the fact that Mom's a journalist, she managed to get the people at the Art Institute to tell her that the man who copied the *Lucretias* was registered as Reinhold Roemer of Essen, Germany, and the man who painted in the National Gallery was registered as Hans Velder of Antwerp, Belgium. Both men had used a passport for ID. Mom told Lucas and me that getting a false passport is easy, especially in big European cities, and they were probably forged.

Next Mom wrote to Scotland Yard, which is like the headquarters of the Police Department in London, enclosed a copy of one of Lucas's drawings of Gallery Guy, and told the whole story about Gallery Guy and the two guards. Scotland Yard wrote back to say, in a very polite way, that the death of Albert Robinson (that was Bert's name) had been ruled an accident, the case was closed, and our letter didn't give them enough of a reason to open it again.

It was all incredibly frustrating. So much for trying to do the right thing.

# Paris, and What We Saw in the Herald Tribune

Lucas and I were eating dinner together one night in June when Mom told us she was going to take a trip to France and Italy later in the month, she'd already checked it out with Lucas's parents, and Lucas and I would be going along.

So by the last week in June we were in Paris, staying at a small hotel. Mom was busy with some fashion stories she had to do, and Lucas and I were hanging out. So far we'd been in Paris five days. It was Thursday. Tomorrow and Saturday Mom was doing a "Paris Looks," and on Sunday we were leaving for Italy.

Ah, Paris. My favorite city. The Luxembourg Gardens with its mothers pushing baby strollers and its patches of flowers. The Champs-Elysées with its busy traffic, sidewalk cafés, and beautiful trash cans. The Eiffel Tower in the

evening, seen from a boat on the River Seine. The minia-
ture Lady Liberty, reminding us where New York Harbor
got its statue in the first place. French bread. Etcetera,
etcetera.

We'd walked around the part of town where all the
really expensive stores are. We'd been to the Louvre, the
world's biggest museum, where we made a special trip
to look at the Rembrandt paintings, and to the Musée
D'Orsay, a museum where they have thousands of works
by Impressionist painters like Renoir and Monet. We'd
climbed to the very, very top of Notre-Dame Cathedral.
One night I ordered shrimp and it came with the all the
heads still on, the little dead eyes looking straight at me.

Thursday morning we were taking it easy, lingering
over our breakfasts, as they say. For breakfast in a Paris
hotel you usually get your choice of the very best café
au lait in the entire world—I like it even without whipped
cream and sprinkles—tea, or hot chocolate, plus croissants
and little loaves of French bread still warm from the bakery, and butter and jam. You can't imagine how good it is
until you taste it.

So there I was, drinking the last of my café au lait
and eating my bread and writing in my journal. This was
a whole new journal book for me because I'd completely
filled up my other one when we took our trip to London.

Lucas was eating her croissants and drinking her hot
chocolate. She'd finished what she was writing. She always

writes so little that she was still using the same blank book Mom gave her before our first trip. Now she was reading the *International Herald Tribune*, which is like the main newspaper for Americans living and traveling abroad. It has news from all over Europe and the world, and lots of news from the United States.

Suddenly she said, "Hey, here's something about Grandma Stickney."

Lucas turned the newspaper my way, and on the front page I saw a picture of a huge crowd of women standing in front of a big building. Most of the women were waving banners in a lot of different languages. The caption under the picture said, "More than 80,000 women gather in Geneva to call attention to women's rights in the developing world."

After I'd seen the picture, Lucas read, "'Women from more than ninety nations are gathered in Geneva, Switzerland, this week to draft a resolution urging greater international attention to the issue of women's rights in developing nations.'

"Blah blah blah, it goes on about Africa and the Middle East," Lucas continued, "then it gets to the part about Grandma Stickney.

"'Margaret O'Hara Stickney,'" she read, "'of Saint Paul, Minnesota, spokesperson for the group International Women United, said, "The size and energy of this gathering is intended to bring attention to the continuing problem of inequality between the sexes, especially in developing countries.'" Blah blah blah. 'O'Hara is among a dozen women selected to present the completed resolution to the United Nations General Assembly in New York in September.'"

"Cool," I said. "The United Nations! That's awesome."

"It's not the first time she's spoken at the United Nations," Lucas said quite casually, not even looking up, as if it was something everybody did once a month or so. I wondered why I hadn't heard about this United Nations thing before, and I figured I'd ask her about it as soon as she finished the article. Her family is really something.

"Let's see," she continued, "it goes on talking about the resolution they're writing, and the story is continued on page five. . . ." She leafed through the newspaper. "Okay, here's—"

She broke off and just stared at the newspaper for a minute, and I swear, her face actually turned white right in front of my very eyes.

"What's wrong?" I said. I thought it was something awful about Grandma Stickney.

"Ho . . . ly . . . shmack," she said, very quietly and very slowly, and she folded the page and handed it to me.

There, at the top of page three, was a headline that said, PAINTING BY REMBRANDT DISCOVERED IN AMSTERDAM CANAL HOUSE, and underneath, in a smaller headline,

*Rijksmuseum Officials Verify Art Discovery of the Century.*

Beneath that was a big photo of the new Rembrandt painting that had been found. It was a picture of a woman I recognized as the Lucretia I'd seen in the other paintings, lying on a bed, dead, with three men and a woman around her. At the foot of the bed was a little black and white dog. There were lots of pillows and messy sheets. The woman was wearing a loose blouse trimmed with gold lace covered up by a gold velvet vestlike thing partly fastened up the front.

And here was the most interesting thing. The woman's hands lay on her stomach, the fingers intertwined.

We'd seen those hands before. We'd painted those hands.

The caption beneath the picture said, "Rembrandt's *Third Lucretia*."

24

# What the Story Said, and Manipulating Mother

The story and picture took up most of the page. Here was the deal.

There was this guy named Willem Mannefeldt who'd died six months before, when he was sixty-seven years old. The Mannefeldt family had made a lot of money back in the seventeenth century selling tulips, and the Mannefeldt company was still selling tulips all over the world. Willem was the head of the company, so he was very rich. He had two children by a previous marriage who inherited his part of the business and most of his money. His third wife, Marianne, who was thirty-two, inherited his house and everything in it.

The paper called the house "one of Amsterdam's finest residences." It was on the "exclusive" Herengracht, which is Dutch for *Gentlemen's Canal.* (By the way, you already know that Amsterdam is in the country called the Netherlands. Well, the Netherlands is also called Holland, and their language is Dutch. Confusing, I know, but that's the way it is.)

Earlier in the summer, Marianne had decided to sell the house and move to the south of France, so she started having people come in and look over everything in the house to tell her how much it was worth.

They found a bunch of old paintings, which they sent out to an art expert. He took them all out of their frames to look at them, and on the back of this one big, ugly painting that had been in the attic, he found something he thought was a painting by Rembrandt.

When this guy told Marianne what he'd discovered, she took it to the Rijksmuseum to have them examine it. (I found out later that *Rijksmuseum* means "National Museum" in Dutch, and that *Rijks* rhymes with *yikes*.) A guy there, whose name was Jacob Hannekroot, was a world-famous expert on paintings by Rembrandt. He examined it with all sorts of tests of how old the paint and the canvas were and other things, and finally he said it was the real thing.

Marianne said the painting should stay in the Netherlands, so she sold it to the Rijksmuseum for what they called an "undisclosed sum." Experts thought the museum probably paid more than twenty million dollars for it.

According to the paper, the newly discovered painting finished off the story of Lucretia. The article told about the Lucretia legend, and about the other two paintings of her. They even mentioned the Minneapolis Institute of Arts. The *Third Lucretia* showed her husband, her father, a female servant, and an unidentified man standing around Lucretia after she died and her body was put on her bed.

The article said that this painting was quite different from the first two, because instead of being "portrait" shaped, which means longer up and down than wide, this one was "landscape" shaped, or horizontal. It also said that this one had what they called "conventional symbolic elements," including the little dog, a mirror, and a candle in the background. Mostly Rembrandt didn't include a lot of symbols in his paintings, so this was unusual for him.

At the end, the story said the painting would be on special display at the Rijksmuseum through October, shown as part of the museum's permanent collection.

"We have *got* to get to Amsterdam," I said to Lucas.

"Right away."

"Without going to Italy."

"Absolutely," Lucas answered. Then we both were quiet while we broke off little pieces of bread and croissants and stared at the walls of the hotel breakfast room, thinking.

By lunchtime we had a plan. We were meeting Mom at a little park in a neighborhood called the Latin Quarter. That whole part of town is covered with tourists in early July, and there are all kinds of food stands where you can buy a good-tasting lunch that doesn't cost a billion bucks. Food in Paris restaurants is unbelievably expensive, and paying for me to go along on her trips meant Mom was always traveling on a tight budget.

Anyway, I saw Mom coming, and when she got up to us, before we even had a chance to say hello, I said, "Mom, did you see the *Herald Tribune* today?"

"Not yet," she said. "Should I have?"

Lucas and I smiled at each other. "You will not believe what we have to show you."

"Okay, show me," she said.

"Not until we have our food and sit down," Lucas said. The paper was in her backpack.

"Hmmm," Mom said. "Am I going to like it?"

I looked at Lucas. "I'm not sure *like* is the right word. I guarantee you'll be surprised."

We walked through the narrow, crooked streets to our favorite Greek food stand, and came back to the park with huge gyro sandwiches and fries and bottles of mineral water.

When we sat down, Lucas, who had the newspaper in her hand already opened up to the right page, handed it to Mom. Mom put it in her lap and, holding her sandwich in both hands, turned aside to take a bite so she wouldn't drip yogurt sauce on the story. When she turned back and started reading, it took about three seconds before her mouth stopped chewing. Still with her eyes on the page, she reached for her bottle of water, took a drink, and swallowed.

At last she looked up at us and opened her mouth as if to say something. While she was still trying to figure out what to say, Lucas put her travel journal on top of the newspaper, right next to the picture of the *Third Lucretia*. The journal was open to the page where Lucas had drawn the hands we'd seen in the middle of Gallery Guy's canvas.

Lucas pointed at the drawing in the journal. "You saw the painting we did of the hands. Well, here's a drawing I made of them while Kari was busy doing the painting."

You didn't have to be an art expert to see that the hands were exactly the same as the hands of the dead woman in the *Third Lucretia*.

Mom looked back and forth at the two of us again, still couldn't think of anything to say, and turned back to finish reading the article.

Finally, when she'd finished, she put down the paper and said, "Good Lord. So what he did was go to Minneapolis to get Lucretia's face right. . . ."

"Mm-hmm," Lucas said, and I nodded.

"And then he went to London to work on the hands."

"Exactly," Lucas said.

"And who knows what other museums he went to for the other parts," I added.

"This is very, very big stuff you two have gotten yourselves into."

I said, "Mom, we've got to go to Amsterdam."

She looked at me for a minute. "I know you'd love to see that painting—so would I, for that matter—but I have an assignment in Italy to complete. Besides, exactly what would we *do* in Amsterdam?"

"Lucas and I talked about this, and here's what we're thinking. There's got to be something more going on than just what's in the newspaper. I mean, how did Gallery Guy's forged painting get into that house on the Heren . . . Heren . . ."

"Herengracht?" Mom said.

"Yeah. Whatever. And if Gallery Guy was doing this for the money, which it makes sense is why he *was* doing it, then what good does it do him if the Rijksmuseum gives all those millions of dollars to Marianne what's-her-name?"

"Yeah," Lucas piped up. "And if the Rijksmuseum has these experts, how come they couldn't tell the difference between a real Rembrandt and a fake? Face it, there's no way we're going to convince anybody that Gallery Guy forged that painting if we don't know any more about all this stuff than we can figure out from sitting here reading the newspaper."

"At least we could go to the museum and *see* the painting," I said. "And we think they'll have lots of information in the museum about finding the painting. Museums always do that kind of thing."

"I suppose you have a point," Mom said, "but *The*

*Scene* is expecting me to cover the fashion collections in Milan. I can't just up and change my plans."

"I'm sure you could come up with stories in Amsterdam that are as good as the ones you're planning to do in Italy," I said.

"Besides," Lucas added, "if we have to, we could maybe extend the trip for a few days. Go to Amsterdam first, and go to Milan after that."

It was time for our big ending. I started. "Mom, ever since I can remember, you've wanted to write for one of those intellectual magazines you think are so cool. The ones we always have around the house. Think of it. You said yourself, this Lucretia business is big stuff. This is your chance, Mom."

"They'd love this story!" Lucas chimed in. "Imagine the headline." She looked up and gestured into the air, as if she were seeing the headline written there. "They'd call it, like, 'How I Helped Two Teenage Girls Uncover the Art Rip-Off of the Century.'"

"Yeah, Mom," I concluded. "All we have to do is go to Amsterdam, where we can follow all this up and prove the *Third Lucretia* is a fake. Then you'll be able to write all about it and sell the story for really big money to *The Atlantic*, or *Harper's*, or *Vanity Fair*."

Mom had put her gyro sandwich down on the bench next to her after that first bite. Now she picked it back up, took another bite, chewed and swallowed, all the time staring off into space like she was thinking. Then she took a third bite, and a fourth, still staring and thinking. First I figured she was thinking of travel schedules. Then, because it was taking so long, I thought she was trying to figure out how Gallery Guy had pulled off the forgery, or what to tell *The Scene* about not going to Italy.

But finally, when she spoke, what she said was, "Not to mention *The New Yorker*."

# 25

# A Train Ride, Amsterdam, and My First Big Mistake

I overheard the conversation Mom had with her boss at *The Scene*. She told them she'd had an e-mail from a friend who was covering the fashion shows in Italy, and that this year's designs were either boring or so far-out no teenager would go near them. Mom told the editors she thought *Scene* readers would be more interested in a story about this hot young Dutch designer who had a new line of clothes for teenagers that was going to be in the department stores beginning in the fall.

I was pretty sure Mom hadn't gotten any e-mail about the Italian shows, and that she'd just made up the story like Lucas and I had made up our stories when we were in London. I thought about telling her that if it was a lie, I was going to have to ground her. But I didn't. Mom has a good sense of humor, but I wasn't sure she'd think that was as funny as I did.

True or not true, Mom's story worked. The editor said okay.

Mom decided to hurry up everything she was doing in Paris so we could get to the exhibit on Sunday. Then she called an old friend of hers who lived in Amsterdam, an American guy named Bill, to ask him to recommend a good hotel. Finally, she called the person at *The Scene* who's in charge of making travel reservations to switch all the arrangements, and by Saturday afternoon we were sitting on a train, heading north to Amsterdam.

This was totally awesome, because it was a high-speed train, which goes hurtling along at almost two hundred miles an hour. It's way more exciting than riding in an airplane because you can see how fast you're going just by looking out the window.

The only thing on the train trip that had anything at all to do with our mystery was that we went through Antwerp, which was the place Gallery Guy said he was from when he was painting in the National Gallery. But we didn't even have time to get out.

Mom lived in Amsterdam her first year out of college, before she married Dad, and she spent the last part of the trip telling us about how it was back then. I guess even before she lived there it had started being Drug City, which it still is, pretty much, because drugs are legal there. Anyway, back then kids would come with backpacks from all over the world and hang out at this place called Dam Square and buy and use drugs. Mom said she didn't do that. She'd managed to get a job as a waitress in an American-style restaurant just so she could stay in Amsterdam, which she loved, and lived a regular life. I don't know if I believe her. Bill, the guy she'd called about the hotel, was somebody she'd met back then.

When Mom got done telling us about this, Lucas said, "So. About this Bill guy. Do you two have some kind of romantic thing going?"

"Well, at one time in my life, believe it or not, there were men. Relationships. Romance," Mom said, and she got a far-off look in her eyes, hamming it up. For the next few minutes she told us how she and Bill had met, dated for a while, then decided to be just friends, and how they'd stayed friends even though they'd both gotten married to other people. Now they were both divorced, but as far as Mom was concerned, romance with him wasn't in the cards.

"But he's a great guy," she said. "He had something scheduled for tonight and couldn't meet our train, but you'll have a chance to meet him while we're here. I think you'll like him."

It was seven o'clock when we got into Amsterdam.

It's hard to imagine how different all the cities in Europe look from each other until you go there. Compared to London and Paris, Amsterdam is like another whole world. It has these canals running through it in U shapes, one inside the other. There's also a big river right in the middle of things. They have streets, too—it's not like Venice, where everyone goes around in boats. But everywhere you look in Amsterdam, there's water.

Kind of at the very top of the town, above and in the middle of all the Us of the canals, is the incredibly big, monstrous, humongous Centraal Station, where we came in on the train.

When you come out of the train station you're on a big plaza where all kinds of things are going on. That night there was a guy with an accordion, a Caribbean drum group, and some man Mom said was from Turkey doing a weird whirling dance in a costume with a big skirt and tall hat. Mom says it's always like that. What a place.

Well, that's just the beginning. When you look down the main street from the Centraal Station you start to see the buildings that Amsterdam is famous for. You've probably seen them in pictures. They're old and tall and skinny, and they have pointed roofs that mostly have little decorations on them. They're on both sides of all the canals and the river, and you can see their reflections in the water. Amsterdam has to be the most picturesque place I've ever been.

Anyway, since we were traveling light and had our little rolling suitcases, we decided to take a tram to our hotel, which was down in a quiet section where they have the big museums and the concert hall. Trams, or streetcars, are like small trains, and they run everywhere in Amsterdam on tracks in the streets.

By the time we got settled in our hotel and went downstairs to the restaurant to have something to eat, all we had time to do was take a quick walk around the neighborhood before it was time for bed. We were all beat. Traveling is hard work.

The next day we were some of the first people in line outside the Rijksmuseum waiting for it to open.

You go into the museum through a gigantic entry passageway that runs completely through the building. As usual, I was busy with my journal, so instead of standing in line with Mom and Lucas, I was on a bench out in the sunshine. Mostly I had my head down. But once, when I looked up, I caught a glimpse of a good-looking blond man walking into the passageway.

It would be easy to say I didn't think anything of it at the time—after all, I only saw him from the back. But to be honest, I have to admit that watching him walk and move, I was sure he was somebody I should know. I wondered if he was an actor or a rock star or something. But he was dressed up in a suit and tie and carrying a briefcase, so I figured he worked at the museum. I finally decided that the reason he seemed familiar was because he looked a lot like Sting, only with longer hair. I picked up my journal again and kept on writing.

If I'd watched him, I might have seen him stop and look closely at Lucas and then at Mom. But I didn't watch him, and I didn't see him do it. And that was a big, big, big mistake.

# 26

## The Third Lucretia

"This does not look good," Mom muttered, her eyes darting back and forth over the crowd behind us as we waited to get into the museum. I'd come over from my bench because it was getting close to opening time.

"I have a feeling we're going to get trampled," Mom continued. "Just look out there. It's a teeming sea of humanity." The crowd stretched all the way through the passageway and out into the plaza.

"Listen," Mom said, "we need a strategy." She turned away from the crowd and motioned for us to huddle near her.

Talking softly so nobody else could hear, she said, "This isn't going to be like Minnesota, where everybody keeps their place in line. Amsterdam is a very cool city, and the Dutch have many good qualities, but Amsterdammers are famous for being pushy.

"Even as we speak, I'll bet four out of every five of those people in line behind us are figuring out how they can elbow us out of the way and be the first to see the *Third Lucretia*. We'd better make a run for it. When they open the doors, we move. Got that?"

We nodded.

"First, we get in front of *Lucretia* and do some serious gazing. Then we fan out. I'm pretty sure there'll be panels that'll tell about other things. Like the story of Lucretia and the two other paintings in the States, and all that."

"We don't need to spend our time on that," Lucas said. "We know that stuff."

"Exactly," Mom said. "Let's each of us look for something more interesting. Anything that tells about finding the painting or figuring out that it was a real Rembrandt, that kind of thing. Okay?"

"Then what do we do?" I asked. "Shall we call each other over? Or just read it ourselves and make a report?"

We all looked at each other.

"I know," Lucas said. "How about if we each read our own panels and only call each other if there are interesting pictures?"

"Great idea," Mom said. "Just in time, too. On your marks . . ."

There was a sound behind the entry door, and suddenly we were let in.

"Go!" Mom said, and the three of us took off, almost

but not quite running, down into the gigantic entrance courtyard where we showed the tickets Mom had bought online, then through another part of the building and, finally, into the special exhibit room.

And there she was. Lucretia.

Because we'd come so fast, we had her all to ourselves for a few seconds, and being alone there with her was totally awesome for me.

First when I saw the painting, just the look and the size of it made me want to stop in my tracks. I couldn't stop for more than a second, of course, or I would have gotten trampled and ended up nothing but a grease spot on the Rijksmuseum floor. But it was the kind of scene that, like, took a person's breath away. And suddenly I got all emotional, feeling lots of things at the same time.

The painting was set up to look dramatic, with no other paintings in the exhibit room, and low lighting with a big spotlight on the picture, which was huge.

And, as I said, there Lucretia was. Looking just like herself, with her reddish brown hair and light gold skin, and the sad mouth with the dark shadow at the corner on the side we could see.

Only she was dead, and everything in the painting seemed very still and quiet and mournful.

Which brings me to another thing I was feeling, which was sadness for the dead Lucretia. Okay, call it silly, but it turned out that Mom had the same feeling, and she said it was a sign of how well the picture had been painted that it could make a person feel truly sad that the woman had died. I think I felt it especially, because I'd always loved the *Lucretia* paintings, and she was like a real person to me.

Then there were the hands. The closer I got to the painting, the more familiar those hands looked. When I finally saw them close up, I actually recognized the brush-strokes. And for a minute I had this incredibly confusing feeling that it wasn't Rembrandt's painting hanging there, or even Gallery Guy's. It was my painting. After a few seconds everything went back to normal, but I didn't stop feeling like I was part of that painting, somehow. I wondered if Lucas felt it, too.

"Lucas," I whispered, "recognize that spot of pink on the first knuckle, and the yellow on the side of the thumb?"

She nodded and grinned at me.

I looked for a while longer at the hands, and at the cute, sad-looking little black-and-white dog at the foot of Lucretia's bed. And at the people standing around the bed, looking as sad and quiet as they would have looked in real life.

Then the crowd got to be too much, and it was time to move on.

Mom was right. There were panels around the walls of the room. Each one was about something different, and they were all written in Dutch, with translations in English,

French, German, and some Asian language. Mom was already busy reading one of them. Lucas had gone all the way to the one farthest away from the painting, and now she was looking at the panel next to that.

I passed by the panel called "Who Was Lucretia?" and went on to the one labeled "Identifying a Masterpiece."

Right at the top there was a photo of a tall blond man looking through a magnifying glass at a painting that was lying on a table. It was the guy I'd just seen outside the museum. He still looked like Sting, but he also seemed familiar in other ways.

I looked hard at his face. At his cheeks, at his ears, and I looked a lot at his nose. And then I knew who it was.

You guessed it—Gallery Guy. Only the words under the picture said, "Jacob Hannekroot, Curator of Dutch Art, Rijksmuseum."

That gave me the shivers, I can tell you that. I quick turned to look for Lucas and Mom, but I couldn't see them because of people in the way. Before I left to go get them, I couldn't help reading what was on the panel and giving the picture a closer look.

With the beard, slicked-back black hair, and the glasses he'd had in London, Gallery Guy hadn't looked especially gorgeous. But it turned out he was a very good-looking guy. In England he'd had brown eyes, but here his eyes were bright blue. I thought he probably was into colored contacts and had both a brown pair and a blue pair, because even if his eyes were naturally blue they couldn't be *this* blue.

He was wearing a pale pink shirt with the sleeves rolled up over his elbows. The shirt was open at the collar, perfectly pressed, and there was something about his posture that made it all look "casually elegant," as they say. He wasn't young, but he looked good.

Just then I heard someone call my name, and when I looked over my shoulder I saw Lucas leaning around some people and gesturing for me.

I fought my way over to where she was standing just as Mom came over from the other side. Lucas had been looking at a panel called "A Dutch National Treasure." It was the story of the Rijksmuseum's decision to buy the *Third Lucretia*, and there was a picture of the museum's director in front of the painting.

But Lucas hadn't called us over to look at him. She wanted us to look at the other people in the picture with him.

There, standing on the director's right, was Marianne Mannefeldt. She was a tall, gorgeous blonde who was totally hot. The dress she was wearing was buttoned all the way up to her neck, but it was tight enough that you could see that she had a fantastic body.

On the other side of the museum director was Jacob Hannekroot, Gallery Guy, dressed in a suit this time and looking just as handsome as he'd looked in the panel I'd been reading a minute ago. Maybe even more handsome.

Lucas pointed at him and gave me a Look—she'd recognized him, too—and I gave her a Look back and moved my head up and down in a big nod.

Mom said, "Now come over and look at this."

She led the way, pushing through the crowd to the panel she'd been reading. There was the story of the Mannefeldt family, a picture of the canal house where the Rembrandt had supposedly been discovered, and a big picture of Marianne with her husband who had died. It had been taken at a party. He was in a tuxedo and she was wearing a low-cut black dress and lots of jewelry. Willem Mannefeldt was completely bald and had a long nose and almost no chin. He looked like a vulture. He had his arm around his wife like she was some kind of a prize he'd won for being so rich and important.

"Not exactly a GQ model, is he?" Mom whispered, pointing to Willem.

"She and that curator of Dutch art guy from the other panel make a much cuter couple," I said, whispering back, and I raised my eyebrows a couple times to let Mom know there was something up.

Mom gave me a questioning look. Then, under her breath, she said, "Makes you wonder how dear old Willem managed to kick the bucket, doesn't it?"

# Figuring It Out

"Are Jacob Hannekroot and Gallery Guy the same person, or what!" I burst out the instant we were through the crowd and walking away from the museum.

"No joke," Lucas chimed in. "Wait till we sit down. I'll draw a picture and show you."

Mom just looked at us. I think she couldn't believe what we were saying. Then she put her finger to her lips and gestured with her head to a group in front of us and people whizzing by on bicycles. Amsterdam is absolutely full of bicycles.

We didn't say any more until we found an outdoor table where our conversation would be covered up by traffic noises. We decided to have lunch even though it was early.

This is probably as good a time as any to tell you about

how to say some of the Dutch names, if you're interested in that kind of thing. *Jacob Hannekroot* is pronounced as if it was spelled YAH-kub HAH-nuh-krote. (Two *o*'s in a row make a long *o* sound in Dutch.) The letter *w* is pronounced like *v*, so *Willem* is pronounced like *Villem*, and *Marianne* sounds like MAH-ree-AH-nuh.

Anyway, as soon as Lucas had taken a quick look at the menu, she whipped out her journal, found a blank page, and started drawing. By the time the waiter had taken our orders, she was almost ready.

"By the way," I said while we were waiting for her, "I think I saw Jacob Hannekroot outside the Rijksmuseum while I was on the bench."

Before anybody had a chance to comment, Lucas turned her journal around and we could see a rough sketch of a man. "That's Jacob Hannekroot all right," Mom said.

Lucas didn't say anything. She just started drawing again. It didn't take her long before she'd turned the drawing of Jacob into Gallery Guy just by adding a beard, slicked-back dark hair, and glasses. She showed it to Mom, then she turned back to the pictures she'd drawn of Gallery Guy when we were in London. The two pictures were identical.

"Well, that's clear enough," Mom said. "Okay, let me get this straight. The Rijksmuseum's curator of Dutch art is the same person who painted the hands on the picture we just saw, which means he probably painted the whole *Third Lucretia*."

Lucas and I nodded.

"And the Rijksmuseum's curator of Dutch art, this same Jacob Hannekroot, is the art expert who then identified the *Third Lucretia*, his own painting, as a real Rembrandt."

We nodded again. Having Mom say this out loud made me feel like holding my breath, I was so excited.

"And the person whose house the phony painting was in is an incredibly beautiful woman whose husband just died, and who insisted on taking the painting to the Rijksmuseum for identification."

"And Jacob is also incredibly good-looking," I said.

"And her husband was old and ugly," Lucas said.

"So Marianne and Jacob were almost certainly in it together," Mom said. She's never chewed her fingernails, but she has a habit, when she's thinking, of taking the nail of her right thumb between her teeth and, like, slowly clamping up and down on it. She did that now. After a minute she said, "What a setup. What an unbelievably smooth, foolproof setup!"

"Except for one thing," I said. "Us." And I broke into a big smile.

Lucas and I were smiling when our food came, but Mom looked more worried than happy about what I'd just said. "Okay, what else did we find out in the museum?" she asked, taking a bite of her quiche.

"Nothing much on my panel," Lucas said. "Just stuff about why the Rijksmuseum decided to buy it. About how

Dutch art should stay in the Netherlands and stuff like that. By the way, it said Marianne has decided not to sell her house here in Amsterdam."

"If you suddenly had a cool twenty million, you wouldn't have to sell any of your houses either," Mom said. "Kari, what was on your panels?"

"Well," I began, "you already know the first thing I found out. That Jacob is the curator of Dutch art who looked at the painting Marianne Mannefeldt brought him and said it was a real Rembrandt. It said he did a test of how old the paint was, then he looked at it to see if it was like Rembrandt's style. He looked at the overall subject and composition and everything. You could say he looked at the *big picture*."

"Ho, ho, ho," Lucas said.

"I'm going to do you a favor and forget you said that," Mom said.

"Obviously you can't take a joke. Anyway, if you know about the other *Lucretia* paintings, you can see right away it's the same woman, so that was the big thing. Then he looked at the way the light came into the painting."

"Rembrandt is famous for the way he painted light," Mom said. Lucas and I already knew this from spending so much time in the Rembrandt room in London, but we didn't say anything.

"A lot of the Dutch painters are," she continued, "like van Gogh and Vermeer—" She broke off because I was giving her my this-is-more-than-I-wanted-to-know look.

"Right. I'll shut up," she said. "You were saying . . ."

"Well, supposedly whoever did this painting—"

"Jacob Hannekroot," Lucas broke in.

"Jacob Hannekroot painted the light coming in from the side just like Rembrandt did in all his paintings," I continued. "And then, get this. This is the most interesting part. There's the thing about the symbols. See, Rembrandt didn't use many symbols, even though lots of other painters did. But in this painting there are symbols."

"The dog stands for loyalty, the mirror stands for either Lucretia's soul or her knowledge of herself, and the candle stands for God's presence," Lucas said.

Mom and I looked at her, figuring this was just one of the millions of things Lucas seemed to know from having read it somewhere.

"It said so on the first panel I looked at," she said, as if she was defending herself.

"Anyway," I continued, "Rembrandt didn't usually use symbols. So what Jacob said was, if this was a forgery, whoever made the forgery wouldn't have used symbols because it wasn't like Rembrandt to use them. *So*, get this, it has to be *not* a forgery, because there are symbols in it, which Rembrandt didn't use."

Mom screwed up her face. "You're kidding."

"That's way complicated," Lucas said.

"That's what was on the panel," I said with a shrug.

"Reverse psychology," Mom said, shaking her head. "This guy thought of everything."

"Then there's the fancy helmet her husband is wearing in the picture," I continued.

"I noticed that," Mom said. "He probably copied that from another Rembrandt painting, in Berlin, or the one in Glasgow."

"And the brush technique."

"We know how he got that," Lucas said.

Mom added, "And he works right here in the Rijksmuseum, where I suppose there are more Rembrandt paintings than anywhere else in the world. He could copy paintings all he wanted. Normally an art expert would have to call in other art experts to authenticate a newly discovered painting, but I suppose Jacob got by with it because he's the world's leading expert on Rembrandt. Who would know better if it was a Rembrandt than Jacob Hannekroot? I'll say it again, what an unbelievable setup."

We were quiet for a minute, letting it all sink in. "You know what makes me sad?" Mom said. "I'm not exactly a certified expert on art, but I've looked at a lot of paintings in my life, and I'd say the *Third Lucretia* is one of the most beautiful works of art I've ever seen. It also has about as much emotional content as a painting could have. I got tears in my eyes. Jacob Hannekroot is obviously a truly great artist. Too bad he doesn't just paint his own pictures and let people enjoy them in galleries."

"But then he wouldn't make twenty million dollars selling a painting to the Rijksmuseum," Lucas said.

"You've got something there," Mom said dryly. "Well, the panel I read just talked about the Mannefeldt family, who they were, how they made their money, and how they might have gotten the Rembrandt to begin with.

"Then it told about Willem Mannefeldt dying and how Marianne started making a list of the belongings in the house. Boy, she and Hannekroot must have had everything planned for a long time, down to the last detail."

"So do you think Jacob and Marianne were lovers before old Willem died?" I asked.

"I'd bet on it," Lucas said. "And I bet he was murdered, too."

"I wouldn't be so sure about either of those things," Mom said. "Just because a man and a woman work together doesn't mean they're lovers. And as far as that and the murder go—well, we might have our suspicions, but let's remember we have no proof of either of those things."

I took another bite of my food. Remembering the pictures of Willem, Marianne, and Jacob, I didn't have a single doubt in my mind that they were lovers. They might not have killed the old guy, Willem—he could just have had a heart attack or something—but that seemed way too convenient.

"I'd like to know how Willem died," I said. "But mostly I want to know what we're going to do about the *Third Lucretia* being a forgery."

"I think we should go to the police as soon as we finish eating," Mom said.

"*Mo*-om, who's going to believe *us*?"

"Yeah, Gillian," Lucas said, "like they're going to listen to two fourteen-year-old American girls and arrest the curator of Dutch art at the Rijksmuseum?"

"You've got a point." She sat for a while staring out at the street and clamping up and down on her thumbnail. Then she said, "Tell you what. We'll just take a nice walk around Amsterdam this afternoon, and I'll think about it."

Lucas and I looked at each other.

"Don't worry," Mom said. "I won't leave the two of you out of it. You're the ones who made all the discoveries, and I'll keep you in the loop on everything. The whole thing is your deal, you know. But from the sound of it, Jacob Hannekroot is about as dangerous as they come. Remember those museum guards."

Remember what happened to Lucas on King's Road, I thought. But I didn't say it.

"And you need some adult help in figuring out what steps to take without putting yourselves in danger."

Maybe so. But somehow Mom seemed to be right in the middle of everything now. Part of me liked having her in on it, helping us figure things out. When she was sitting there talking about Marianne and Willem and Jacob a few minutes ago, she made me feel like the mystery we'd discovered was a big deal after all, just like my intuition had said it would be. And I knew that Jacob Hannekroot was an extremely dangerous guy, even more than she did, so I couldn't blame her for wanting to keep us safe. *I wanted us to stay safe, too.*

But danger or no danger, part of me still felt that the mystery belonged just to Lucas and me. And that part didn't like having Mom in the middle of things at all.

# Mom's Not-So-Great Plans, and the Bad Part of Town

Amsterdam is not a big city. At least the parts of it that tourists want to see. You can actually see a lot of it in just a few hours. By five o'clock we'd walked through what I suppose you'd call their downtown and down a long pedestrian-only street with shops, and we'd seen about a thousand canals, a few hundred cute little bridges, and a billion canal houses, including the one where Marianne lived and the painting had been found. We'd avoided at least two million people on bicycles, and seen at least a billion more bicycles lined up outside every big building, tied to every railing, and on bike racks at every street corner.

We finally settled down to have a snack in my mom's favorite little bakery, which she says has been selling the best almond butter cookies in all of Amsterdam since way back when she lived there.

When we were sitting at a corner table with our coffee and cookies, Mom said, "I've been thinking."

I braced myself. Thinking is often a dangerous thing in a parent.

"About your mystery. I agree the police would never believe our story because we don't have any real proof, so we have to count them out. And I don't want to go directly to someone else at the Rijksmuseum. They'd probably not believe what we told them anyway, and besides, they'd be sure to tell Jacob, and we can't have him knowing. Jacob is a killer.

"But somehow we have to plant doubt in the mind of some art-world honcho that Rembrandt painted the *Third Lucretia*. I think we need to go to somebody in the United States. I've interviewed the director of the Minneapolis Art Institute for a couple of stories, so he knows me. What I'll do, if it's okay with you guys, is call him tomorrow and tell him about this. I would suppose he knows somebody at the Rijksmuseum, and he'd probably be willing to call or send them an e-mail or something to say he has reason to believe the painting is a forgery and suggest they get some outside experts in to authenticate it. And I'll make sure Jacob never knows the tip came from us, so we won't be in danger when he learns his crime is going to be found out."

I didn't say anything and neither did Lucas.

"Don't all cheer at once," Mom said. "What's wrong with my idea?"

"It's just so . . . so boring!" Lucas started. "I mean, here we've had all this adventure figuring out the mystery and everything, and now you're just going to call this guy in Minneapolis and let him take it from here?"

"Well, I don't know of any other way to approach it. I thought we might try to get an appointment with some big official at the museum, but it occurred to me it might not be safe to do that. We don't know if there's anybody else in on the forgery besides Jacob and Marianne. If we told somebody else, and that somebody happened to be in on it, we could be in actual, physical danger. We're going to have to be extraordinarily careful. The only person I can think of who can help us that we know is absolutely safe is the director of the Art Institute."

Mom waited for our reaction, but we still didn't say anything.

"Look, you guys," Mom said, "you've done some great detective work, and you can be very proud of that. But to be honest, I'm not sure I should have brought you here to Amsterdam. I'm beginning to think this whole situation has way too much potential for danger. Tell me one thing. In London, when you were watching Jacob Hannekroot, did he ever get a good look at either one of you? Did he see Lucas when he said 'Go a-*way*' to that little boy?"

"I was kind of behind him when that happened, and he didn't even look at me, or we couldn't have spied on him," Lucas said. That much was true, and it's what I'd told Mom after our flight back from London.

I was still looking at Lucas, waiting for her to tell Mom about the argument she had with Gallery Guy, when all of a sudden I felt a kick in the shin so hard that I actually yelled, "Ow!"

"What's the matter?" Mom asked.

"I just bit my tongue." This was not a lie. Lucas's kick had surprised me so much that I actually had bitten my tongue, but it didn't hurt enough to make me yell like that.

"Oh, I hate when that happens," Lucas said, totally innocent. "But anyway, that's the closest we came to having Gallery Guy see us," she continued, ignoring my dirty look.

"Well, even so, I'm worried about your safety," Mom said. "We think Jacob may have killed at least three people. He's utterly ruthless. It scares me to death to think what he might do to you if you got in his way. Even if he never saw you, I want the two of you to keep a very low profile while we're here. Understand?"

We both nodded.

"Tell me you won't try any funny stuff," Mom said.

We were both quiet.

"*Tell me,*" Mom said, in her Parent's Voice of Authority.

Finally we both muttered, "Okay," but I'm sure Mom could tell we weren't very happy about it.

She was obviously still considering the situation, because she took another sip of coffee and said, "I think the two of you should probably stay close to me while we're here."

"Oh no!" Lucas wailed.

I said, "Please, Mom, we'll keep out of Jacob's way. What are we supposed to do—sit around in waiting rooms while you do your interviews? That would stink! We'd be totally bored. Totally!"

She looked down at her coffee, then up at us.

"Well, I don't want you going anywhere near the Rijksmuseum. Got that? My first obligation is to keep you two safe, and if I thought for one minute—"

"Don't worry, Mom, we'll be careful."

"And we won't set foot in the museum. Honest, Gillian," Lucas added.

"Promise me." She looked really serious now.

"We promise," I said.

"Okay, I trust you." She gave a big sigh, and shifted in her chair. "Well, here's what I'll do. It's Sunday. I'll call the Art Institute tomorrow right after nine A.M. Central Time. That'll be, let's see, four tomorrow afternoon here. How about if I tell this guy the story and ask his advice on what we can do from this end to get the *Third Lucretia* looked at by other experts. I'll also ask Bill if he knows of anyone here in Amsterdam who could help us out. Okay? Is that better than just letting the Art Institute director handle it?"

Lucas and I looked at each other and finally nodded.

When Mom looked down to break off a part of her cookie, I tried to catch Lucas's eye to see how she was reacting to all this.

But I couldn't, because she was staring in the other direction, thinking her own thoughts.

It was after we'd walked for a while longer that Mom started telling us about the bad part of town. It came up because we were waiting for a tram at a place called the Rembrandtplein, which is a little square with a statue of Rembrandt and a bunch of other guys in the middle of it. This square is surrounded by nightclubs and bars that completely light the place up with neon signs at night. On some of the side streets, some places had advertisements on them that said *Peep Show* or *Sexy Girls*, all in English, I suppose so tourists from all over the world can read them.

"Is this the bad part of town?" I asked.

It seemed like a good question, but Mom gave a slow chuckle and shook her head. "Oh, this is mild for Amsterdam. The really bad neighborhood is just up there a few blocks." She pointed in the direction of the peep-show places toward a part of town we hadn't seen at all that day. "It's called the Quarter. They have a lot more of this," she said, gesturing to one of the clubs with a picture of a dancing girl on the side, "and much, much worse."

I was going to ask what, but just then the tram came. It

was six thirty on a Sunday night, so there weren't a lot of people riding the trams. We got a whole area in the back to ourselves.

"The Quarter is probably pretty dangerous these days. *Everywhere* seems to be more dangerous these days, and it was bad enough when I lived here."

"Back in medieval times," I added.

As I said, this all just came up in conversation. It didn't seem any more important than any of the other things Mom had said that day, like about the tulip trade that was so big in the seventeenth century, and how the country is actually below sea level and the land was created by using dikes to block out the water, and how everybody in the Netherlands speaks English plus three or four other languages.

But it turned out to be a really, really important conversation. Because before we left Amsterdam, we were going to end up spending a lot of time in the dangerous part of town.

## 29

# My Second Big Mistake

The next day, Mom spent the morning calling to schedule appointments and interviews for *The Scene*. Then she tried to get an appointment to interview Jacob Hannekroot for a magazine story. At least that's what she *told* them. But they said he was in meetings and she'd have to call back the next day.

By afternoon she had left to do some work, saying she wouldn't be back until six, and Lucas and I were alone for the first time in days.

It felt really good. I love my mother. Honest. But spending too much time around her can get very old.

Lucas and I decided to go see the Anne Frank house, the place where she hid from the Nazis and wrote her diary. I won't go into it, but it was pretty depressing. I kept thinking about some school friends of mine who are Jewish, and what would have happened if they'd been alive and over here during Hitler's time.

After that, to cheer ourselves up we went to the Hard Rock Café Amsterdam and we each had a hot-fudge sundae. We'd gotten most of the way through the ice cream and chocolate sauce when Lucas said, "You know how your mom said she'd call the guy from the Art Institute?"

"Mm-hmm," I said, scooping up the last bite.

"How much do you want to bet this whole thing with him just drags on and on?"

"What do you mean?" I was looking in my bowl, wondering how the sundae could be gone already. Even though I was stuffed, it tasted so good I could have eaten another one right then and there.

Lucas was still working on hers. "Well," she said, gesturing toward me with her spoon. "First of all, it's summer, and he might be out of town. If he's there, he's probably busy." She stopped to take a bite. "Then, do you think he's going to be able to take her phone call or call her back right away? I doubt it. Who knows when she's going to be able to talk to him? It's going to take forever." She looked down and started scraping the side of her dish.

"You're probably right. Nothing is ever as easy as you think it should be, especially when it comes to adults." We were quiet for a minute. "Are you thinking what I'm thinking?"

"That we should do some detecting of our own?"

"Exactly."

"What do you have in mind?"

"Well, we promised my mom no going into the Rijks-museum, and no funny stuff. But we didn't promise her that we wouldn't keep an eye on Marianne."

"Marianne? Why would—" Lucas began.

"Here's the thing I've been thinking about," I broke in. "Remember when we were with Mom and looking for Marianne's place, and her house ended up being on the other side of the canal from where we were?"

Lucas nodded.

"Well, remember that little outdoor café that was just about where we were standing when we realized we needed to go over to the other side?"

"Yeeeaaaah?"

"Well, what if we went and sat at that café and took your camera and watched her door, and ended up getting a picture of Gallery Guy—Jacob whatever-his-name-is—going into her house? Or better yet, a picture of them kissing on her doorstep? Remember when Mom said we didn't have any proof they were in a relationship? Well, that would be awesome proof. And it would help in our case when the police finally get involved. Which they will eventually, once somebody figures out the *Third Lucretia* is a forgery."

Lucas gave me a sideways glance and her face broke into a little smile. "Not a bad idea, Kari Sundgren. Not bad at all."

"It's five after four now. How about we go over to that coffee shop and just hang for a while. Marianne's house is so close to the museum that if Jacob leaves work at five, he'll be there before five thirty. That's not so long."

We were on our way, walking down the street, when Lucas said, "The more I think about it, the less likely I think it is that Jacob will turn up. He's been super sneaky in everything. I don't think he'd come to visit his girlfriend at her house."

"Still, we'll be doing *something*," I said. "And that beats sitting around doing *nothing*."

But we hadn't been at the café for more than ten minutes when something did happen, only not what we expected.

When we'd gotten there, the coffee shop was just like I remembered, with cool house music piped outside and the smell of coffee spreading all out to the sidewalk. We sat down at a table where we had a good view of Marianne's blue door through the trees planted on both sides of the canal. Lucas was wearing her camera around her neck. She took it off, pulling the strap over her head, then, as casually as possible so people at the other tables wouldn't notice, she flicked it on, fiddled with the zoom lens, and set the camera down on the edge of the table. The digital screen on the back showed a perfect picture of the blue door with the number over it, and just enough of the surrounding building to prove that it was for sure

Marianne's place. If Jacob showed up, we were all set.

The waiter—Heri, according to his name badge, which I figured must be pronounced like *Harry*—was probably in his twenties, had spiky bleached hair, and spoke almost perfect American English. After we gave our orders he disappeared through the café door. A few minutes later he came out with a tray with all the stuff on it.

"Here are your hot chocolates," he said, and started putting things down on the table: cups, two small pitchers of hot chocolate, and a plate with two little cookies. While he poured each of us some hot chocolate from our pitchers, he said, "And where in America are you young ladies from?"

I answered, "Saint Paul, Minnesota."

Just then he looked down at the camera with the picture of Marianne's door showing, but he didn't mention it. Instead, he said, "Isn't Saint Paul near the source of the Mississippi River?"

Lucas was asking how he knew so much about America when I happened to glance across the street. And there was the blue door wide open, and the woman whose picture we'd seen in the Rijksmuseum was coming out, a big canvas shopping bag over her arm.

"Holy meep!" I said, and I scooted my chair back on the concrete so fast it practically fell over backward. "Lucas, grab your stuff, we've got to go."

I slung my backpack over my shoulder while Lucas

got the camera strap around her neck. "How much do we owe?" I asked.

Heri, who'd been looking way cool all this time, suddenly looked confused.

"But you haven't drunk—"

"How much?" Lucas piped up, using her firm voice.

"Five euros."

I reached in my pocket, found a five-euro bill (they don't leave tips in Europe), flung it on the table, and off Lucas and I went, running on our side of the canal to catch up to Marianne, who was far ahead of us now, only on her side.

I looked at Lucas as we ran. "Stupid us. Why didn't we think of this?" We'd prepared for Jacob coming to her door. But like idiots, we hadn't prepared for Marianne going anywhere.

Lucas ignored me. She says it's not a good idea to "beat up on yourself." Instead she said, "We've got to get to the other side of the canal. Let's do it up there." Still running, she pointed to where a big cross street went over the water.

Gorgeous Marianne with the great body had incredibly long legs, wouldn't you know it, and she walked fast, so she was still ahead of us when she got to the bridge. But as it turned out, we didn't need to cross over to her side. She took a left on the big street and crossed over the canal to our side—ended up walking practically right toward us, in

around when he heard our chairs scraping as we sat down. When he saw us, his eyes got wide in surprise, and just for a second I thought I saw an expression that was definitely not friendly.

Before he could say anything, Lucas said, "Two hot chocolates, please."

"Are you going to drink them this time?" he asked sarcastically.

"Nobody likes a wise guy," Lucas said.

"Is that an American expression?" Heri asked.

Lucas and I both nodded.

"'Nobody likes a wise guy.' I'm going to have to re-member that one," he said. Then he hoisted the tray of dirty dishes up to shoulder height, and off he went into the café.

This time when he came back and started to put our stuff down, he asked if we'd had to rush off to a fire.

Lucas said, "No, we thought we saw somebody we knew. But she got to the flower market before we did and got lost in the crowd."

That look I thought I'd seen in his eyes returned. "So you know Marianne Mannefeldt?"

I caught my breath, but Lucas said, "Is that who she was? We thought it was our friend."

"Hmm," he said, now pouring our hot chocolates out again. "I thought you had a good chance to see who she was when you stopped by the side of the canal up near the Vijzelstraat. I must have been mistaken. Marianne's a regular customer here." There was nothing friendly in his voice or his eyes now.

I waited for Lucas, hoping she'd come up with one of her instant lies, but even she couldn't seem to think of a likely story. So we stayed quiet while Heri finished pouring our drinks, put the tray under his arm, and disappeared inside.

Somehow the hot chocolate didn't taste very good after that. While we sat there, I wondered why it hadn't occurred to either one of us that Marianne might leave her house, or that she might sometimes stop in at the coffee shop nearest to where she lived.

Maybe you could call it beating myself up, but I personally felt totally stupid when I thought about everything that had happened.

When Heri came out again we asked for our bill, paid it, and left. The minute we were back out on the street and headed toward the hotel, I said, "I'm sorry. This was all my idea, and it wasn't a very good one. We didn't find out anything about Marianne and Jacob. And the first time we were there he saw your camera was on and pointing at her door, so he knows for sure we were spying on her. What if he tells her about it—maybe even tells both her and Jacob? What if he describes us?"

"So what? They don't know who we are."

I wanted to ask what would happen if Jacob heard about us, put two and two together, and figured out Lucas was the same girl who'd been trying to see his work in London. But I knew she'd think that was as ridiculous as thinking he'd been driving that Jaguar that had almost hit her.

And another thing: all this time, I'd felt like I was a lot safer than she was because Jacob didn't know what I looked like. But now, with Heri maybe describing me to Jacob, I felt a little less safe. But even if Lucas didn't make fun of me for my theory—and I knew she would—I couldn't exactly ask her to feel sorry for me, since she'd *always* been in danger from Jacob.

So all I said was, "It still feels like a mistake."

"It's true it didn't work out," Lucas answered. "But I think your idea of getting a picture of the two of them together wasn't stupid at all. In fact, I think it was pretty brilliant."

But she was wrong and I was right. As it turned out, my idea of keeping watch on Marianne from a coffee shop on the Herengracht was my second big mistake.

# Keeping a Tail on Jacob

When we got up in the morning, it was raining. Since we'd been really busy for the past few days, Lucas and I decided just to hang.

The hotel had a little TV lounge downstairs with comfortable chairs. Nobody else was around, so we watched some British sitcoms on the BBC, then listened to our iPods.

We also got to know the owners of the hotel, a couple named Tony and Miesje. Tony was tall and handsome for an old guy, and had silver hair. He was always dressed in a blue blazer without a speck of dust on it, and his gray pants always looked like they'd just been ironed. Miesje (whose name was pronounced MEES-yuh) was quiet and blond. Tony spoke perfect English, but Miesje's English was pretty basic.

It was the middle of the afternoon when Lucas said, "Kari?" She had that sound in her voice again, the one that means she's going to try to get me to do something that might end up getting us in trouble, and she wanted me to approve of it.

"I'm still here," I answered.

"You know what a good idea I thought it was to try to see Jacob and Marianne together?"

"Mm-hmm."

"I think there might be another way to get a picture of them meeting. Or if they don't meet, at least to learn a little more about Jacob."

"Is it going to get us in trouble with Mom?"

"No, nothing like that."

I must have looked like I didn't quite believe her, because she said, "Remember, yesterday I went along with your idea to spy on Marianne and I never complained about it once."

She was right. Fair was fair. So I said, "Like, what exactly were you thinking?"

Finding out what we needed to know from the Rijksmuseum was easy. All we had to do was make a phone call. Yes, of course she spoke English, the receptionist said. The museum would be open until six o'clock, but the administrative offices closed at four thirty. And the museum's curators worked in a small building in the courtyard behind the museum.

We didn't need disguises, but we wanted to blend into the crowd. So we wore jeans and our hoodies, because the weather was cool and rainy. Lucas had her backpack over her shoulder. Even though we were kind of young, we thought we looked like any of the thousands of kids who flock into town every summer from all over the world.

We found out from a guard which building the curators used, and which door they'd use to leave. I kept watch on that one. Lucas stood near the passageway in case Jacob took a tunnel or something into the main building and came out through the public entrance. We could only hope he wouldn't leave from some other door.

Another thing we didn't know for sure was if he'd go home at four thirty. One of the million things Mom had told us during our walk was that the Dutch get weeks and weeks of vacation every year and they're less likely than Americans to stay late or come in early.

We hoped Jacob was that kind of guy.

At 4:31 on the dot, people started coming out of the entrance I was watching. Then, for about five minutes, they came out in bunches. Then they straggled out. And at 4:43, one of the stragglers turned out to be Jacob Hannekroot.

He was dressed in a tan raincoat with the collar up. The belt was tied instead of buckled around his waist. His shoes were shined. He had a black umbrella that popped up automatically when he pushed a button. He had great posture, holding his shoulders up high the way I'd seen other European men do, and he walked like he had somewhere to go. He carried his leather briefcase with a long strap over his shoulder. I wondered if his briefcase was full of forgeries.

Lucas and I both followed him, but she and I had decided to stay apart. We figured if he thought he was being followed he might try to lose us, or even come right up and tell us to "Go a-*way*!" But if he did that to one of us, the other could keep on following and find out where he went. And if anything more dangerous than that happened—not that we thought anything dangerous *would* happen—the other would be more able to help if she wasn't in the middle of it.

Besides, although I didn't say this to Lucas, I was still worried about what he might think if he saw us together— after what Heri might have told him.

We were hoping he'd go to Marianne's place—Lucas had her camera and I'd bought a disposable camera in case I was closer than Lucas when we saw Jacob and Marianne together.

First he walked to a nearby tram stop. When the tram came, he got on in the second car. There were five cars, and I got into the third one. I didn't know where Lucas had gone.

It was rush hour, and a lot of people were getting on. I had to stand in the aisle and hold on to a post. I couldn't see Lucas, but if I stuck my head out far enough over the people who were sitting down, I could see the back of Jacob's head, tilting down as if he was reading something.

Two stops up, we passed right by the place where we'd followed Marianne the day before. If he'd wanted to go to her place, he'd have gotten off there. But he didn't.

On the whole trip, I got only one glimpse of Lucas, who turned out to be in the last tram car. We'd been traveling for what seemed like a long time, and I was wondering whether we were going all the way to the Centraal Station when I saw Jacob's head come up and a corner of a newspaper as he folded it. He stood up and headed for the door. I headed for my door, too.

It was Dam Square. A minute later Jacob was moving around through the groups of kids hanging out, with me behind him and Lucas bringing up the rear.

Jacob was tall and walked fast. It had stopped raining and was just drizzling a little. He looked up at the sky, held out his hand as if checking for raindrops, then gave his half-folded-up umbrella a good shake, as if he'd decided it wasn't worth putting it up again.

We'd followed Marianne the day before, but that was only for a couple of blocks. This time we were walking for a lot longer than that. I've seen enough movies and TV shows to know how to follow somebody without being spotted. The only times I had to duck into doorways or pretend to look in shop windows was when he waited to cross a street. Otherwise he never even slowed down, and he never once looked back. I didn't know what he'd do if he saw me, but if my theory about Heri was true—and my intuition told me it was—I didn't think it would be good.

A couple of times I saw Lucas behind me when Jacob and I were waiting at corners. Otherwise I was too busy following to keep track of her. I had to almost run to keep up.

In fact I was so busy staying behind Jacob and avoiding people on bicycles that it really didn't occur to me where we were going until I saw a guy just lying in the middle of the sidewalk with his eyes half open. This was also like something I'd seen on TV—people totally spaced out from using drugs. Then I started looking around and it suddenly hit me. We were heading for the Quarter.

No, I was wrong. We were *in* the Quarter.

# A Near-Death Experience

Those first few blocks in the bad part of town didn't seem so awful. Yeah, it was drizzly and gloomy and there were some weirdos like the guy on the sidewalk. But there were also fast-food stands and flower stalls, and even little flower boxes on the buildings, just like in other parts of town. Plus, the place was filled with people doing regular tourist things like taking pictures and eating french fries from little cups.

I was still feeling okay when we turned left onto a street that ran by a canal. The street sign—which, like most street signs in Europe, was on the side of a building—said OUDEZIJDS ACHTERBURGWAL. I was just thinking what a weird name this was for a street when I looked down into the street itself and started to feel nervous.

This was like places I've seen in previews for the kind

of movie I never want to go to. There were buildings advertising sexy girls everywhere. There were stores right on the street where you could buy drugs. Men huddled together on corners talking. It seemed like men were everywhere, alone and in groups. Most of these guys ignored me, but two of them said things to me in languages I didn't understand. A bunch of guys in U.S. Navy uniforms said something creepy to me in English that I don't even want to repeat.

There were a lot of women standing around, too, and some teenage girls. Most of them weren't dressed for the cool weather and they didn't have umbrellas. They must have been freezing. I thought the women at least would be nice, but when I passed them they nudged each other and looked at me. One of them said, "Little American girl should go home to Mommy." I didn't know how she knew I was American.

The only thing that saved me was knowing that Lucas was around. I took a quick look over my shoulder, but I couldn't see her.

It had been almost two blocks since I'd turned the last corner. She should have been on the street behind me by now. I made sure Jacob was still in front of me, stopped, turned around, and gave a good long look up one side of the street and down the other. I waited to see if she came out from behind somebody or reappeared from a doorway. Nothing.

Lucas just plain wasn't there.

My heart gave a lurch, and suddenly my mouth felt dry. In the whole time we'd been spying on Jacob and solving this mystery, Lucas and I had always been together. Even when we went separately into the Rembrandt room at the National Gallery, I always knew where she was.

Suddenly I thought about the Jaguar that had almost run over Lucas in London and I stopped dead in my tracks. Had the same thing happened here? Had nobody been there to scream at her and save her life? I turned around and took about three steps back the way I'd come before I remembered that the one person who would try to kill Lucas was Gallery Guy, and he was walking in front of me.

I turned back around and had to run to catch up. As long as she didn't get hit by a car, I figured I didn't need to worry about Lucas. The streets we'd been on were extremely busy, and Mom always told me that, except for traffic accidents, busy streets are safe streets.

But I *was* worried about *me*. I was alone, following a murderer in a really bad part of town—a murderer who might know I'd been spying on his girlfriend the day before. And where Jacob and I were heading there weren't as many people on the sidewalks, just closed-up buildings and lots of trash everywhere. If Lucas wasn't around, was it smart to keep going?

Jacob was half a block ahead of me when I saw him take a right. I decided I'd just go around that next corner, and if it kept on looking lonely and scary down there, I'd turn back.

I half walked, half ran to catch up, glad my tennies didn't make any noise. But it wasn't the running that made me breathe fast and my heart pound in my ears—I was scared.

Maybe it was intuition, maybe it was fear, but something made me slow down when I came to the street where Jacob had turned. I took a deep breath and stepped around the corner.

And there he was. Right smack in front of me, opening a door. Five more steps and I'd have run right into him.

I froze. Absolutely stopped moving. Stopped breathing.

Jacob hadn't seen me—yet—but as close as I was, he *would* see me when he looked up from turning his key. And when he did, he might kill me.

I knew I should run for my life, but I couldn't move. Couldn't even breathe. I stayed there, rooted to the spot. It was like being in a nightmare.

Then, just then, I heard something. Music. At the other end of the block, the sound of a bunch of drunken men singing a song I'd never heard in a language I didn't understand, then the sound of breaking glass.

The crash brought me back to reality. Jacob turned to look where the sound had come from, and in that instant I pulled back around the corner, ready to run—

And there was Lucas. Closer to me than I'd been

to Jacob a minute before, and when she spotted me she opened her mouth to say something.

No time to say *shh* or put a finger to my lips. I jumped toward her just as she said, "K—" and I clapped a hand over her mouth, spun her around by the shoulders with my other hand, and pulled her up, her back to me, my back to the wall. She reached up to pull my arm away, but I just grabbed her hand and held her tighter.

One second, two seconds, three seconds—it seemed like forever. Then, at last, I heard Jacob's door slam.

I sagged, let go of Lucas, closed my eyes, and breathed for what I swear was the first time since I'd gone around the corner.

"What the . . . !" Lucas exploded. I let her rant while my heart slowed down.

At last I was able to say, "I almost ran right into Jacob! He just went into a door!"

"Well, I think a couple of my fingers are broken." She started to massage her hand. I hadn't realized how tightly I'd squeezed until I saw her fingers were all white and stuck together.

"Where the meep were you?" I asked.

"I was hiding from Heri."

"Heri the waiter? He was here in the Quarter?"

"Yeah, he was walking around, all alone."

"Did he see you?"

"I don't think so. The minute I saw him I stopped

and pretended to be looking into a window, but he might have."

She didn't seem to be bothered about this, but I groaned. I wondered if Heri knew Jacob well enough to know he had a place in this part of town and, if he'd seen Lucas just a few blocks away from it, if he'd tell him that we weren't just spying on Marianne, we were spying on *him*.

"Which is Jacob's door?" Lucas asked. As usual, she was totally calm.

"The one right around the corner. You can't see it from here. But Lucas, I could have been . . ." I was going to say "murdered."

But before I could tell her how scared I'd been, before I could say that this was really, really dangerous, she said, "Well then, let's go where we can have a look."

Still rubbing her hand, she calmly walked across the little empty street to the opposite corner and stood under a sign that said MISSION OF ST. MARY MAGDALENE, A SAFE PLACE FOR WOMEN, and what I figured was the same thing in Dutch.

"What, are you crazy?" I hissed. "What if he sees us?"

"You think he's going to start staring out the window right after he gets up to his room? No way," she said.

The street Jacob's place was on was like others I'd seen in Amsterdam. They're like regular streets, with buildings on each side and front doors and things, except they're not wide enough for a car to get through. Mostly they're a way for pedestrians to get from one normal street to another. In the center of town they're full of shops and restaurants. But this one was just an empty, narrow alley with ugly, depressing buildings. The only interesting thing was the mission, which had curtains with the kind of lace trimming they have a lot of in Amsterdam.

Jacob had gone into what looked like a warehouse. It had a pointed roof without any decoration. The windows were especially big, and an outside staircase, almost half as wide as the ministreet itself, crisscrossed the front of it. I remembered something Mom had said, that in Amsterdam, stairs like this were meant for loading, so bulky things could be carried into and out of the big windows on each of the floors because the stairways inside were too skinny.

The buildings were so tall and the street so narrow that it was almost dark. As we watched, a light went on in the top window, five floors up.

"Let's climb up the stairs and look inside," Lucas said.

"Lucas! No way! This has been dangerous enough! Besides, it's six o'clock. Let's get out of here. We have to be back at six thirty." I looked hard at Lucas. I knew she wanted to stay and explore, but I wasn't going to back down on this one.

When I started walking back the way we came, she said, "Okay, okay, but we've got to come back here. Maybe tomorrow."

"Lucas, I could have been killed! Don't you understand?"

"Next time we'll stay together," she said.

I couldn't even think of anything to say. Sometimes her nerves of steel grate on my regular ones.

We were lucky. The tram we needed pulled up as soon as we got to the stop. It was only about ten after six, and I knew we'd get back with time to spare.

It wasn't until we were sitting in the tram that my near-death experience hit me and I started shaking. I had to keep my mouth shut tight so my teeth wouldn't chatter. I wondered if this was how Lucas had felt in London when she was almost run over.

Lucas wasn't looking at me at first. At last she turned around to say something, opened her mouth, stopped, and said, "Kari, are you okay?"

"N-n-not especially," I said. And right there in the tram Lucas gave me a big hug, and it helped. I stopped shaking.

# 32

# Bill, Rijsttafel, and Arguing in Bed

Back in our hotel I got a Coke on the way up to our room, and after I'd drunk most of it I started feeling almost normal. Lucas and I were lounging around, looking very casual, when Mom breezed in, saying, "Hi, guys, what's new and wonderful?"

We told her about watching TV and taking a walk in the rain. It felt like London again, covering up what we'd done. I realized that what had happened to me was exactly the kind of thing Mom had been worried about, and why she'd made us promise no funny stuff.

"Did you get hold of the guy at the Art Institute?" I asked. I thought changing the subject might make me feel less guilty.

Mom stepped out of her shoes and flopped down on her bed, her hands behind her head. "Well, I got through to the Art Institute. The director's on vacation. Believe it or not, he's taking a boat trip up the Amazon. He won't be back until next week."

Lucas gave me an I-told-you-so look.

"So what are we going to do?" I asked.

"We'll ask Bill at dinner if he knows of anybody who can help us."

I'd totally forgotten about going to dinner with Bill.

"By the way, he asked if I'd go with him to a concert tomorrow night. I told him yes. I figured you guys would love to have an evening free of your elderly traveling companion."

It didn't take an Einstein to figure out that from that moment on Lucas was thinking of what we were going to do during our evening alone.

Bill was medium height and had straight, shiny dark hair and big brown eyes that made him look kind of like a sweet little puppy.

He took us to an Indonesian restaurant—there are lots of them in Amsterdam, because Indonesia used to be a Dutch colony—and we had something called *rijsttafel*. It turned out to be a big bowl of rice surrounded by thirty-six little bowls of stuff to go on it, like meats with different kinds of sauces, lots of vegetables and pickles, fruit, nuts, and toasted coconut. You put whatever you wanted onto your rice. It was fun.

When Bill went to the men's room, Mom asked, now that we'd met him, if we'd feel comfortable having her tell him what we'd found out about the *Third Lucretia*. We said yes. Bill was the kind of guy you could trust. So when we were walking home and there was absolutely nobody around who could hear us, Mom told him. He seemed very impressed.

"Do you want to be the one to break this story in the newspapers?" he asked Mom.

"No, I'm not a reporter anymore. I just want to write a background feature piece I can sell to a magazine."

"Then I know exactly the person who can help you," he said. "Johanna Heimstra. Works for one of the big dailies here. Always after a good story. I'll give her a call in the morning. I won't tell her much, just that it's a major scoop and she has to talk to you."

"How much do you want to bet Bill can't reach his friend?" Lucas whispered into my ear when we were lying in bed. Mom sleeps with earplugs, so we can usually get by with whispering to each other if we're careful to make almost no noise at all.

"Probably on vacation on the Riviera," I answered.

"Or climbing in the Alps," Lucas said.

"Exploring Norwegian fjords by sea."

"Sitting on an Egyptian pyramid."

"In India studying yoga."

"So," Lucas whispered after we'd kept this up for a while, "when are we going back to visit Jacob's house?"

"Are you nuts? I'm not going back there! You don't understand. If it hadn't been for those drunks singing and throwing a bottle down at the end of Jacob's street, I'd probably be dead by now! And if Mom had found out, she'd have me cut in little pieces and dropped into a canal. Besides, it's just a stupid thing for girls our age to do. End of story."

"Listen," Lucas said. "I understand how scared you were. But if we plan it out—"

"Lucas, I'm not sure anymore that Jacob doesn't know who we are and that we're here. I know you don't believe me, but I still think he was the one driving the Jaguar in London. . . ."

I could feel her take a breath, ready to say something about this, when Mom said, "What are you two whispering about over there?"

"Nothing," I said. The good old standard, all-purpose line.

"Well, keep it down. I'm trying to get some rest here."

"I'm not going back over there, and that's final," I breathed into Lucas's ear.

"We'll talk about it in the morning," Lucas breathed back.

# One Last Chapter Before
# We Get into Trouble

There was a message to call Bill when we got back upstairs from breakfast.

Venice. That's where his friend was. Venice. She was doing a story on how they're trying to keep their buildings from sinking into the water. Her boyfriend said she'd be back in town on Friday evening.

We hadn't thought of Venice.

"We'll just have to wait," Mom said. "Remember. The *Third Lucretia* isn't going anywhere. We're not going anywhere, Friday will be here soon enough."

Easy for her to say. It was only Wednesday. Friday seemed like twenty years away.

The minute Mom was out of the hotel, Lucas took up our conversation exactly where we'd left off the night before. "Look," she said, "if we don't get this last little piece of evidence, we don't have a very strong case about Jacob being Gallery Guy."

"What last little piece of evidence? Besides, I think we have a very strong case." I was pretty sure I was being conned.

"Well, what do you think we're going to find in that place in the Quarter? You think Jacob lives on that ugly little street? Jacob? With his fancy clothes and his big-deal job?"

I thought a minute. At first I thought she meant that Jacob might use the space to meet Marianne. But I couldn't see a woman like Marianne, who was used to having big bucks, sneaking over to meet Jacob in a building that might be full of rats and spiders.

Finally I figured out what Lucas was getting at. I remembered how big the windows were, and that his apartment was on the top floor where the light probably shone in. "It has to be his studio, where he does his painting."

"Exactly."

"What do you think he's working on—another forgery?"

"Who knows? Maybe. But if we can tell that reporter or the cops or whoever that Jacob Hannekroot has a secret art studio at such-and-such an address, and if we can tell them that in that studio there might be studies for the *Lucretia* painting, or even other forgeries that he's working on, then we'll have him for sure. It'll be even better than catching him and Marianne together. The case will be as good as proved."

"We have a lot of evidence *now*! How about the hands we painted? That canvas is in the States, on my closet shelf. We had to have painted it from what we saw in London, and those hands are the hands in the *Third Lucretia*."

"But somebody else could be painting them right now from pictures of the *Third Lucretia* that must be in all the magazines this week."

"Are you kidding? As careful as I was to paint it like Rembrandt? You couldn't get that from a magazine picture. Besides, what if Jacob catches us this time? Even if he wasn't the one who tried to kill you in London, he's still dangerous. He killed those museum guards."

"He's not going to kill us right across the street from a mission, for goodness' sake. Besides, it'll be night and he'll be gone. Artists don't paint at night. They need daylight."

"He was at his studio last night when it was dark enough he had to put a light on."

"Yeah, but that was way in the back of his apartment. The bathroom or whatever, not toward the front. He's on the top floor. If he works by the window, I'll bet he was able to paint for at least another hour, even though it was cloudy. Anyway, we'll wait till it's a lot darker and we'll make sure there aren't any lights on in the building. And we'll take a flashlight. If we find out it really is his studio, it's just what we need to prove the whole thing."

"So what if it is? And what if he's even in the middle of forging another painting? How do we get the authorities to believe us? Besides, what'll we tell Mom? Honestly, Lucas, I don't want to seem goody-goody or anything, but I'm really getting tired of lying to my mother. It makes me feel . . . not very good. I was already grounded for three weeks after the London thing."

"I don't like it either. I wouldn't so much mind lying to *my* mother, but your mom's different. This will be the last time. I promise. The last thing we do that we have to cover up."

I wanted to ask her how she knew, and how long this promise covered—a week? a month? a year? Instead I said, "What are we going to tell her if we find something?"

Lucas sighed and turned her head to stare at the wall. "I haven't quite figured that out yet. But we'll come up with something. We always do."

"Suppose we go to Jacob's place, and suppose he's not there. What if he has friends in the neighborhood? Somebody in one of those bars farther down the block, or a neighbor. Or in the mission! What if somebody says to him, 'You know, Jacob, I saw these two girls looking at your house the other day,' and he asks them to call him on his cell phone if they see us again."

"We'd better wear black."

"They'll still see us! What if he comes after us?"

"We've outsmarted him before, Kari. We can do it again. But I think it would be better if we didn't look so different from everybody else who hangs out around there. I wonder how we could look like we fit into the neighborhood."

After a minute I said, "You know, I think I have an idea."

Somehow at the time I didn't even realize I'd lost the argument. That's what happens when I try debating with Lucas.

So we went out and spent some of Lucas's money. We met Mom for lunch, and in the afternoon we helped her with an "Amsterdam Looks" in front of a big department store.

When we stopped for sandwiches on the way back to our hotel, Mom announced that she had very big news. She'd gotten an appointment to see Jacob on Friday at two. She couldn't see Marianne Mannefeldt until Saturday morning. She figured she was going to be able to put together an awesome feature story on the forgery after Bill's friend broke the news in her paper.

"Does that mean we'll be in it? Your story, I mean?" I asked.

"Of course! You'll be the stars!"

Lucas and I looked at each other and smiled. It would be sweet to be the stars of a magazine story, even if it wasn't the kind of magazine our friends would read.

That night Bill was going to pick Mom up at six thirty for a glass of wine, then they were going to hear an orchestra performance at the Concertgebouw, which was the big concert hall near our hotel. After the concert they were going to go out to supper somewhere.

"What are you going to hear?" I asked as I ate my salami sandwich on a little bun. I didn't care about the music, of course. I was just leading up to some time-and-place questions, but I had to work them into the conversation.

"I don't know. It's the Concertgebouw Orchestra. I don't even know who the soloist is. I just hope it isn't music by some composer I can't stand, like Schoenberg or Schumann. I don't think I could take it tonight. I'm beat."

"Are you and Bill going to some special restaurant afterward?" I tried to make the question sound as casual as I could, but it seemed like I was grilling her.

I was surprised when Mom answered me back as if she thought I was really interested. "Yeah, kind of. We're going to the restaurant at the American Hotel. It's an extremely cool place."

I'd seen the American Hotel on the Leidseplein, the square where the Hard Rock Café is. It was in the other direction from the Quarter.

Lucas and I looked at each other. Mom would be safely out of the way until midnight.

Back in the hotel while she was getting ready, Mom said, "Now, you're sure you'll be all right?"

"Mom, we're just going to take a canal tour. What can happen?"

She reached into her purse. "Here's some money for the boat, and you know where you can catch it, in front of the Rijksmuseum. And don't go into the park. It's dangerous at night. After the tour I want you to come right back here. Got that? And be sure and stay together."

"We'll stay together every single minute," Lucas said firmly.

And we would. Part of the deal we'd finally made was that we'd be together the whole time. If I was going to go back into the Quarter and check out Jacob Hannekroot's studio, I wasn't going to let good old Nerves-of-Steel Stickney out of my sight.

# Sister Anneke, Sister Katje, and Mom

Walking into the quarter this time, I didn't have to have a near-death experience to feel like I was in a nightmare. Neon signs lit up the night sky. People stared at us as we walked along. The air smelled disgusting, noisy music blared out of the bars on both sides of the street, and up ahead a drunk guy was standing with a beer bottle in his hands yelling in Dutch at the top of his lungs.

Even with Lucas beside me, I was scared.

Like I said before, in the daytime the first part of the Quarter seemed pretty friendly, almost like a tourist attraction. Now, with all the stores closed, it seemed like a place where only bad things happened.

Both of us had put on lots of eye makeup and lip liner, and we were wearing short black skirts and tight tops, black nylons and black shoes, all of which we'd bought at a cheap shop up in the central part of town. Even with our jeans jackets, we totally fit into the neighborhood. All except for the shoes. The women around here wore high heels, but we needed flats.

I suppose it was our outfits that made the men act way too friendly. It didn't take me long before I started wondering if dressing up like the women who hung out in the Quarter had been such a good idea.

I noticed a couple of women staring at us from half a block away. Even though it was night, and cool, they were wearing short, strappy dresses. They had on a lot of make-up and high-heeled shoes. It wasn't until we were almost next to them that I saw they were really young, not much older than Lucas and I were. It was obvious just looking at them that they were tougher than I'd ever thought of being.

Still, I felt sad that they were here, in this awful part of town. This was worse even than what I'd seen in those movie previews, and it was way worse than I'd expected it to be. I knew the whole world wasn't Mr. Rogers' Neighborhood, but I hadn't imagined it being quite like this. The guys scared me. I was sure some of them were on drugs, and that scared me even more. Even the women kind of scared me.

What I did to get through it was just focus on walking. Step step step step step. Focus on getting as far as that bar entrance up ahead. On getting past that guy with the long, greasy hair slumped over in a doorway. I left the men and what they said to us to Lucas, who seemed to ignore it.

If Jacob's corner on the Oudezijds Achterburgwal had been in the very busiest section, I couldn't have taken it. But at night it seemed like a *good* thing that it was quieter there. There weren't any weirdos around, which made it feel safer. I also was keeping my eyes peeled in case Jacob was on the street somewhere, but when we got closer and the street got emptier, it was obvious he wasn't. In fact, the only people we saw while we were walking the last block before Jacob's corner were two women going into the Mission of St. Mary Magdalene across the street from Jacob's place. There were lights on in the mission, but it seemed quiet.

When we got to the ministreet, Lucas marched around the corner and plopped her backpack down on the sidewalk. She seemed to have forgotten to check if Jacob was around.

Not me. I hadn't forgotten for one minute. I went across to the mission side and looked up at his window. No light. In fact, there weren't any lights on in the building at all. The more I looked at that ugly building in that dirty little street, the surer I was that Marianne Mannefeldt wouldn't set foot in it in a million years. Of course Jacob could be up there alone taking a nap or something, but at nine thirty at night that didn't seem very likely. I was pretty sure he was gone.

I walked back to where Lucas was taking off her jacket.

"Are we sure this is such a hot idea?" I asked.

"What? What are you talking about?"

"Standing around looking like the women who hang out here," I added.

"You're the one who wanted to dress up like this in the first place!" Lucas said, and reached out for my jacket. I took it off and gave it to her, and she stuffed both of them into the backpack.

"But I'm thinking maybe it was a mistake," I said. Actually, I was thinking that on a scale of one to ten, this idea should get about a minus eleven.

"Well, it's too late now," Lucas said.

By this time we were finished getting rid of our jackets and we each had a heavy flashlight. We could use them for light, but we thought they'd also be good to use as weapons in case anybody tried to do anything bad to us.

We were dressed in black so we'd be less noticeable— especially Lucas, who was going to climb up the outside stairs to look in Jacob's window. Lucas and I had decided that I'd stay at the bottom and keep watch while she climbed up because I'm afraid of heights. In fact, just thinking about going up there made me feel sick and dizzy.

While I was looking at the front of the building, I noticed the address of the place. Jacob's place was number 17, and above and to the right of the door was a street sign that said ACHTERBURGWALSTEEG.

The staircase must even have seemed high to Lucas. She looked up, took a big sigh like she was going to do something she didn't want to do, and whispered, "Here I go."

"Wait a second. What do I do if somebody comes out of the mission?" I asked.

"Say you're just hanging out. You have a right to be here."

"What if some men come up and start—"

"Tell them to drop dead. Don't worry."

"But what if—"

"*Stop worrying, Kari!*" Lucas hissed.

She turned to the staircase again and took another look up. I moved out to a place on the sidewalk where I could keep watch on both the Oudezijds Achterburgwal and the little Achterburgwalsteeg. Just as Lucas put her foot on the bottom step, the mission door opened and a woman came out.

It wasn't one of the women who'd gone in a minute before. They'd looked like they belonged in the neighborhood. This woman didn't. She had dark hair with some gray in it, she wasn't especially slim, and she wore a buttoned-up cardigan sweater, slacks, and lace-up shoes with thick soles like older women wear.

She glanced from one of us to the other and said something in Dutch.

Lucas said, "I'm sorry, we don't speak Dutch."

The woman switched to English. "I said, what are you doing here?"

"We're just hanging out," Lucas said.

"So you are American girls, are you?" It didn't sound mean. In fact, she seemed friendly. She had big blue eyes with nice crinkles around them.

We both nodded.

"What are you doing in this part of town?"

"Are you a nun?" Lucas asked. I noticed she was answering a question with a question, but she kept her voice respectful. Her family's Catholic and she knows a lot of nuns.

"Yes I am," the woman answered. "My name is Sister Anneke. Sister Katje and I founded this mission." She was still right in front of the door. Now she opened it and called, "Katje!" and added something else in Dutch.

A tall, gray-haired woman appeared in the door behind her. "Why don't you come in and have a Coca-Cola or something?" Anneke asked. "Nice girls like you shouldn't be standing outside in the Quarter."

I wasn't sure what Lucas would do, but I knew our plans for climbing the stairs were shot, and I for one didn't want to go inside and have a Coke with a couple of Amsterdam nuns. "Thanks for inviting us, but I think we'd better be going," I said. I quickly walked over to where we'd put the backpack, slung it over my shoulder, and started pulling on Lucas's arm.

"Don't tell anyone we were here," Lucas said. "Please. It's important."

"*Alstublieft*," I said, which is the Dutch word for "please" that we'd learned from Tony. I gave Lucas another jerk, and we turned around and started walking. Partway down the block Lucas said something I didn't quite hear, about how we had to come back later. I just ignored her and started walking faster. There was no way I was ever coming back, and I meant it this time.

We walked fast down the street and through the really bad section until finally we were almost running.

We were almost out of the Quarter, waiting for a traffic light when I looked across the street.

There, waiting at the other curb, was Mom, with Bill beside her. Mom looked us over, starting with our made-up faces, then down to the skinny tops and the short skirts and the black nylons.

We were totally busted.

# 35

# Blaming It All on Arnold Schoenberg

Mom almost never gets really mad. Irritated? Yes. Naggy? Yes. Especially certain times of the month, if you know what I mean. But hardly ever mad, and never, never, never *this* mad.

She didn't say one single word to us all the way back to the hotel. First she said something to Bill, who gave us a look like he felt sorry for us, turned around, and walked away. Mom hailed a taxi and opened the door for us to get inside. Back at the hotel she led the way up the stairs, unlocked the door, and held it while we walked in.

All this time it was obvious she was steaming, boiling mad. Her movements were quick and jerky, and you could see in the light that her face was white. She was shaking.

When we got into the room, she hung her purse over the arm of the chair, took off her coat, and hung it in

the closet. Then she said, "Siddown." Not "Sit down."
*Siddown.*

We sat, perched on the side of the bed. Mom stood
over us, her arms folded tight across her chest.

Then it started. I timed it by the clock radio, which
was on the desk behind where Mom was standing, and it
was twenty-five minutes of solid lecture.

You can about imagine. She started out with, "I can't
believe I found you leaving the Quarter looking like . . .
like that." Next came, "How could you do this when you
expressly promised not to?" "I thought I could trust you."
And, "I thought you had better sense than this."

Then she started pacing and shouting. She told us how
rotten we were for deceiving her, how she could never trust
us again, and how we'd blown the good relationship we'd
had.

Then for a while her voice got intense and she sat on the
chair, teeth clenched, her head sticking out so she was in
our faces. She said if it hadn't been a whole concert of music by Arnold Schoenberg, which both she and Bill hated,
they would have been calmly sitting in the Concertgebouw
and she wouldn't have found out what lying sneaks we'd
turned into. And she wondered what else we'd been doing
in all the years Lucas and I had been together.

After that part was over, she got up again and started
pacing, her arms folded so tightly in front of her that it was
almost like she was hugging herself. "Walking around the

streets in that part of Amsterdam at ten o'clock at night looking like . . . I don't know *what* kind of women." Her voice rose, and she started to sound hysterical. "Do you have any idea how dangerous that was? Do you have any idea what somebody might have done to you?"

It was then she began to cry. With tears running down her face, she said, "You could have been killed, or raped, or . . ." She heaved a huge sigh, then she broke down and sobbed.

I was mad that she was yelling at us like this, and I stayed mad even after she started crying. Yes, I knew we'd done something stupid, something that could get us into trouble if we got caught. But she was overreacting. After all, we hadn't been killed or raped or sold into white slavery. So I just held my lips really tightly shut and stared at the wall most of the time.

Lucas was looking straight at Mom, her chin up high as if she was trying to face all Mom's anger without flinching. Lucas is more used to arguments than I am and they don't bother her a whole lot, but I figured she wouldn't much like being chewed out by my mother.

All this time Lucas and I hadn't said a single word. Now, under my breath, I said, "It's all Arnold Schoenberg's fault."

Obviously the wrong thing to say.

Mom raised her head and said, "Okay, that does it. You two are grounded for the rest of the entire time we're in Amsterdam. You will not leave this room unaccompanied. That's for what the two of you did. Kari, I was going to ground you for three weeks when we got home, but because of that stupid remark we'll make that four. And just for good measure we'll throw in the weekends on either end. That makes it five whole weekends. I'll take your cell phone, and you'll have no phone or IM or e-mail privileges the whole time. Maybe that'll teach you to take responsibility for your own actions. Lucas, I'm going to have to tell your parents about this. They'll have to determine your punishment."

I started to say something, but decided not to.

"It's after eleven now, and I wish we could finish this discussion in the morning," Mom continued, as if it had actually been a discussion, "but frankly, after your behavior tonight, I don't trust you to tell me the truth about anything if you have a chance to consult each other in advance. So tell me now exactly what you were doing in that part of town dressed the way you were and exactly what happened. I want the whole story. Everything." Lucas and I looked at each other. Another mistake.

"*Don't test me,*" Mom hissed through clenched teeth. "Talk. Now."

So we talked. I didn't want to, and when I said something I did it mostly with my lips closed as much as possible. Lucas wasn't as mad as I was, so she told most of it.

We started out telling her about our trip to the Quarter

that night, but we weren't very far into it when Mom said, "How did you know where this studio was located?" I looked at Lucas who, without looking at me at all, told her about following Jacob the day before.

"So where was this, exactly?"

"At a corner on a street we can't pronounce. Owd-something ach-ter-burg-wal," Lucas sounded out.

Mom said something like, "Oud-uh-zites ahk-ter-burg-vahl," correcting our pronunciation out of habit. "Smack in the heart of the Quarter. Whose idea was it to go over there tonight?"

"Mine." Lucas said it firmly, and kind of loud. "And I want to be the one who gets the most punishment. Kari didn't want to go, and I talked her into it. I'm sorry for all the trouble I caused." One thing I've got to say about Lucas: once she's caught, she's never afraid to take responsibility for what she's done.

I'm not always as good at that as she is. In fact, I have to admit I sometimes try to keep from getting in trouble by covering up, blaming somebody, or once in a while telling a little white lie. But Lucas inspired me. "It was my idea to dress that way, though," I said, and I felt good about saying it.

Mom swore, which she almost never does in front of me. "I can't believe it. I can't even believe it." She put her hands over her face for a minute, put them down again, and said, "So, which of you went up the stairs, or did you both go?"

"Nobody went up. There's a mission across the street." We explained about Sister Anneke coming out, and Sister Katje. Mom just kept on shaking her head.

"Get ready for bed," she said abruptly.

So, silently, the three of us got into our pajamas and washed up and brushed our teeth, and one by one we all got into bed, and finally Mom switched off the light. I noticed that she didn't put in her earplugs like she usually does.

I couldn't get to sleep. I could tell that Lucas was awake for a long time, too, and once while we were lying there I reached out and gave her arm a squeeze, and she found my hand and squeezed it back. Then, not much later, I heard her breathing steadily.

For at least a half hour I lay there trying to get over all the feelings I was having. I was still really mad at Mom for putting us through that drama with her shouting and shaking and crying and telling us how she'd never trust us anymore.

Then suddenly I remembered something Mom always says about anger. She calls anger a "covering emotion." She says almost all the time when people get angry they think they're just mad, but mostly, without knowing they're doing it, they're covering up another feeling, like fear or hurt or guilt or grief. Something they'd rather not feel. And then I started thinking about what Mom was probably covering up. Just thinking about how much anger she'd needed to cover her emotions, I figured out how incredibly afraid she must have been when she found out we'd been alone in the Quarter, and how hurt she was that we'd lied to her, and maybe how guilty she felt for leaving us alone.

That helped me understand why she'd been so mad. And after I figured that out, I realized that part of my own anger had been covering up how guilty *I* felt and how hurt *I* was at having lost Mom's trust. For a minute I let it sink in that what Lucas and I had done had blown the good relationship Mom and I had even after what Lucas and I had done in London, and it would take months to earn that trust back, if I ever did. And I started to cry. Then I thought of what a terrible, horrible, no good, very bad night it had been, and all I'd been through since yesterday, and I cried even harder.

# More Grounded Than Usual, and Learning About the Mission

Things were quiet around our hotel room the next morning. But while Mom was taking her shower, I said to Lucas, "Could you believe that lecture last night?"

"We had it coming. We lied to her, we disobeyed her on purpose, we were going to cover up what we'd done, and I suppose we put ourselves in a dangerous situation. We did do something bad, and letting us off easy wouldn't make sense. That's why they give bigger sentences to criminals who do worse things.

"Really, it's me you have to blame," she continued. "I knew we'd get in big trouble if your mom found out, and I talked you into doing it anyway. I'm sorry."

Lucas was working up to being a know-it-all again. I could hear it coming, and I was too tired and sad and cranky to put up with it.

"What do you mean, you knew? Like you're the only one of us who knew, like you're so much more mature or something? I was the one who didn't want to do it in the first place!"

"I said I'm sorry!" Lucas snapped, and just that minute Mom turned off the shower, or we'd probably have gotten into a real argument.

We were quiet through breakfast. All three of us looked tired, and for me even eating took a lot of effort.

The worst moment came when we were back upstairs. Mom said she was going to have Tony, the hotel owner, check up on us every so often, just to make sure we didn't go anywhere. It made me realize how little she trusted us. What made it worse was that I knew we didn't deserve to be trusted.

I took a nap after Mom left, and that made me feel better. About eleven, Tony came up with two Cokes, a plateful of Miesje's cookies, and a stack of books. At one he brought us sandwiches for lunch. I wrote in my journal. Lucas wrote a postcard to a friend. We read and listened to our iPods. It was all very quiet and very boring. I don't know if Lucas and I were still mad at each other or just exhausted or what, but we didn't seem to have much to say.

Mom came back at five and took us for a walk by the canals for a little exercise, and we stopped to eat at a restaurant by the Concertgebouw. Mom said it was an authentic

Dutch place, and we all ordered croquettes, kind of like deep-fried balls of mashed potatoes with little bits of ham in them, which are a Dutch specialty.

While we were sitting there, waiting for our meal, I said, "Mom, I've been wondering about those nuns and what they do in their mission."

You might think this was a stupid thing to ask, since it brought up the whole subject of the Quarter and everything, but Mom also knows some nuns and she really likes them. I thought getting her talking about them would keep her from thinking about what I did wrong.

But I also asked because I really wanted to know. I'd been thinking a lot about the nuns, and the mission they called a Safe Place for Women, and the women I'd seen in the Quarter.

"Interesting subject," Mom said, and I knew I'd been right to ask the question. "I think nuns have always helped out women in trouble, for centuries and centuries."

"But why would those women get in trouble in the first place? I mean, what I can't figure out is how they end up in that part of town, living that kind of life."

"Well, in the old days, of course, a lot of women were thrown out 'onto the streets,' as the saying goes, if they did something disgraceful. Got pregnant without being married, for example. Or if they were caught having an affair, or were raped."

"Like Lucretia," I said.

"Exactly like Lucretia," Mom answered. "I suppose that's at least part of the reason why Lucretia killed herself. She didn't want to have to live that kind of life. Things changed later in the Roman Empire when morals began to deteriorate, particularly among the privileged classes—" She stopped herself, probably because she saw us starting to look bored.

This gave Lucas a chance to say, "There weren't nuns then. That was before Christianity. Christ wasn't born yet."

"Good point. Anyway, it's different today, thank goodness. Women have choices. Nowadays, most of the women you see in the Quarter were probably abused as children."

"Aren't a lot of them runaways?" Lucas asked. "I think I read that somewhere."

"Mm-hmm. And usually they run away from home because they're abused, either physically or sexually. I'd bet ninety-five percent of the women you saw over there come from that kind of background. Don't get me wrong. A huge majority of people who were once abused overcome their past and live good, healthy lives. But a few of them don't. They fight the feeling they're not worth much. So they go and make their life with other outcasts from society.

"As for the nuns, they must feel that God wants them to 'minister to these women,' as they might put it. I'm not sure just what goes on, but I'd guess that the mission is a place women can go to talk and hang out, get something to eat, have a cup of coffee, that kind of thing. Maybe they have a place where women can stay for the night. They might even offer other things for women who want to change their lives, like money and clothes and a place to live."

Just then our food came, and we changed the subject. But for a long time I kept thinking about Anneke and Katje, and what good people they were to spend their own lives trying to help other women make their lives better. I know this sounds weird, but I also wished there had been nuns back in Roman times so that Lucretia wouldn't have had to stab herself.

# What Happened When We
# Went Down to Dinner

The next morning was a lot like the day before. I finished the Agatha Christie mystery I'd started. Tony came and went, and brought us lunch from downstairs. Lucas and I started to talk to each other a little more. We both said how bad we felt about what we'd done and about Mom being mad. I also told Lucas that I hadn't appreciated it when she acted like a know-it-all the day before, especially after she'd gotten us into the whole mess to begin with. Lucas actually apologized. And I apologized for being nasty to her.

The afternoon was better. Earlier in the week, Mom had had this big idea and called Uncle Geoff, who of course has a key to our house, and asked for a favor. She asked him to get our painting of the hands from my closet and send it to us. It came that afternoon, and since we knew what it was, we opened it up while Mom was gone.

Looking at the picture reminded us of our adventures in London, and we started thinking about what it would be like when the forgery was found out. Then we practiced what we'd say to Bill's friend the journalist about how we'd discovered all about Jacob and the *Third Lucretia.*

The morning had started out gloomy, but now it was sunny and pleasant outside. Our room had big European-style windows that went all the way down to the floor. You opened the windows like a set of doors, and you were protected from falling out by a little railing that had a flower box hanging on it. There weren't any screens.

At five thirty we were leaning out over the railing when we saw Mom come around the corner and look up.

"Hey, guys. Whaddup?" she said.

What a relief! Mom was back in a good mood, at least for the time being.

We knew why right away, because when she got upstairs she threw open the door and said, "I have now officially met and had an incredibly good interview with Jacob Hannekroot."

"What's he like?" Lucas said, at the same time I said, "Tell us about it!"

"Well, he's charming," she said, kicking off her shoes and falling onto the bed. "Very sexy, actually, if you didn't know he was a diseased rat. Get this: he said that in his opinion the *Third Lucretia* is one of the most beautiful and powerful of all Rembrandt's works. I about *threw up.*

What a hypocritical, egocentric, self-congratulatory . . ."

"Meep," I supplied.

"Exactly. And he talked about how generous Mrs. Mannefeldt had been to *donate* the painting 'for the good of the Netherlands,' instead of putting it up for public auction. Evidently he calls selling something for twenty million bucks a donation. Oh—and you'll love this—when I told him I'd seen the two *Lucretia*s on display together, he said how fortunate I'd been, that he'd seen both paintings at separate times, but he hadn't been able to find time in his schedule to see them hanging together."

"What a liar!" Lucas said.

"Did he seem like the kind of person who could be a murderer?" I asked.

"I thought about that when I was sitting there," Mom said, "and I guess I have to say I can believe he'd do it. There's something very hard and cold about him, although on the surface he was all charm and polish. He asked about my trip, was I here simply on business or was there an element of pleasure as well, was my hotel comfortable, all that sort of schmoozy thing."

"What did you tell him?" Lucas asked.

"I think I said I had my daughter along, although it was largely a working trip for me. I didn't think it was necessary to mention you, Lucas."

"Anything else?"

"I'll take my notes with me to dinner and go over them to see if I've forgotten anything fun."

The three of us chitchatted for a while longer. Mom said a few things to let us know she hadn't forgotten we were still in trouble. When she got off the bed to start getting ready for dinner she said, "Oh, I almost forgot." She rooted around in her briefcase for a minute, then threw a new *Time* magazine on the bed. "Their story about the *Third Lucretia* is really good. Too bad the painting's a forgery and they'll have to take it all back."

I grabbed it right away and found the page, which of course had a big picture of the painting at the top. The headline said, THE DUTCH DISCOVER AN INTIMATE MASTERPIECE. The writing in the article was hard to understand—like, the caption under the picture said, "In Lucretia, serene heroism coexists with poignant vulnerability." But I could see why Mom liked the story. It said that Lucretia's situation stood for what women had gone through for centuries. It went on about the symbolism, and about how the painting was found and examined and sold to the Rijksmuseum. It called Jacob "the world's foremost authority on the works of Rembrandt van Rijn."

While I was reading, Mom and Lucas were getting ready for dinner. "Tony said they have a big anniversary party coming into the restaurant at seven, and we should get down there early if we want to get served," Mom said. "You'd better hurry, honey."

But I'd just gotten to the part where it said that the work "was painted from the depths of Rembrandt's personal grief," and I wanted to find out about why Rembrandt had been so sad, so I just kept reading.

Finally Mom said, "Kari, aren't you going to join us?"

I looked up, and she and Lucas were standing at the door.

"It's after six thirty, and Lucas and I are ready."

"You guys go ahead and get a table. Order some croquettes for me. I'm at an interesting part. It's talking about how Rembrandt painted the *Lucretia*s at the end of his life when he'd run out of money and after his housekeeper who was also his girlfriend died. As soon as I finish, I'll put my shoes on and be right down."

"*Find* your shoes, you mean," Mom said, looking at my clothes, which were scattered all around my suitcase. "You've got a mess here. When we get back tonight, I want you two to straighten up all your things."

"Yeah, yeah, yeah," I said under my breath as Mom and Lucas left the room.

I finished the article, and it did take me a few minutes to find my shoes. As I was putting them on it occurred to me that, with Mom in such a good mood, tonight might be the night to apologize for going over to the Quarter. I was thinking about this as I ran downstairs and through the hotel lobby into the restaurant.

But Mom and Lucas weren't in the restaurant.

"Have you seen a tall, dark-haired woman and a blond girl about my age?" I asked the waiter.

"Yes, I gave them menus at the table there in the corner," he said, pointing, "then they stepped outside to speak to someone."

"Speak to someone?" I couldn't quite understand.

"Yes, miss, just a moment ago. A gentleman was at the street entrance to the restaurant. He asked me to tell your mother and the young lady that he wished to speak with them. I believe he was a Dutchman. A good-looking man, wearing a raincoat," and he gestured around his waist to indicate a belt. "Your mother asked me to watch her things, so they must be coming right back."

I looked at the table where Mom and Lucas had been sitting. Sure enough, there was Mom's notebook, and her small black leather bag hung over the back of one of the chairs.

I went to the entrance, but the street was completely empty. I couldn't think who would have wanted to speak to Mom and Lucas, or why they weren't still outside.

Then it clicked. Good-looking. Dutch. Belted raincoat. And the purse on the back of the chair.

Mom had left her bag and interview notes because she thought she'd be right back. But she wasn't coming right back. She and Lucas had been kidnapped.

Kidnapped by Jacob Hannekroot, the murderer.

# Rescue, Part 1

It's funny how a person's mind can work in a crisis. Suddenly, without even thinking about it, I knew exactly what I needed to do. What's even more weird is that I was perfectly calm about it.

I went over to the table, grabbed Mom's notebook and purse, and moved quickly and smoothly out of the restaurant, like a shark gliding through the water at top speed. "Where's Tony?" I called to Miesje across the lobby as I opened the door to the hotel.

"Upstairs. Room fifteen. Toilet is—" She broke off, not knowing the right word.

This was a problem, but right away my mind found a way around it. If Tony was fixing the plumbing on the fourth floor, I'd have to find another way to get where I was going. Quickly, calmly, I unzipped Mom's purse and opened her billfold. I could see plenty of European money. I stuffed the money in my pocket, put the purse on the desk, opened the notebook, and, fast as I could, wrote *17 Achterburgwalsteeg.*

"Tell Tony to send the police to that address! Mom and Lucas have been kidnapped!"

"I do not understand," Miesje said, her kind eyes big and apologetic.

By this time I was across the lobby. "Just send the police!" I yelled over my shoulder. Then I pushed through the doors and ran the five blocks to the taxi stand.

I jumped into the first taxi in line. "Corner of Oudezijds Achterburgwal and Achterburgwalsteeg, fast as you can go," I said, trying to use Mom's pronunciation. "I'll give you an extra fifty euros if you can do it in less than ten minutes." It was something I'd seen on TV, but I wasn't sure it would work in real life.

It didn't. The guy just sat there, looking back at me over his shoulder. For a second I thought I hadn't pronounced the words right and he didn't understand. Then he said, "You shouldn't go to a place like that."

I reached in my pocket and held up the fifty-euro bill, worth more than fifty bucks in American money. "My mom's been kidnapped and that's where she is. Now drive."

He drove. Whether it was because he believed what I said or because he wanted to earn the money, I'll never know for sure. We pulled out and around the corner, tires squealing.

For the first five minutes of the trip there wasn't much traffic, and the lights stayed green. Then we hit a red light. It seemed to last forever. I started out drumming my fingers on the armrest, and ended up pounding it with my fist before the light changed. When I saw a second light turn red two blocks ahead I wailed, "Oh, no!" and the taxi careened around the next corner with a right turn that sent the back of the car skidding.

We were on a narrow, cobblestone street. The car shook so badly going fast over the small, rounded stones that I wondered if it might actually break apart.

We were in the Quarter now. The driver put his hand to his horn again and drove, dangerously fast, through the tourists who scattered in front of us. "If I go to prison for this, will you pay the money to get me out?" he asked. I think he was feeling like the star in a movie car chase. But I was way too worried and too busy thinking to answer him.

Suddenly we slowed down, and the driver started looking up at the sides of the buildings to check the street signs. Then we stopped with a jerk, and I recognized Jacob's corner. The ride had taken twelve minutes—two more minutes than I'd bargained for—but when I saw that the meter said twenty euros, I just threw fifty euros into the front seat, said "Thanks a lot," and jumped out. I closed the taxi's door softly behind me so that Jacob wouldn't hear me.

There was light in Jacob's windows. Thank God. I'd been sure this was where he'd take Mom and Lucas, and I'd been right.

By this time I had it all planned in my mind. If I got there before the police showed up, I'd get Sister Anneke and Sister Katje to call and make sure the cops were coming, and the nuns and I would go up to Jacob's place together.

I ran to the mission door, turned the handle—and it was locked. The sign on the door said, *Return at 7:30* in Dutch and English. It was just after seven o'clock.

I felt desperate. I wanted to cry, but I didn't have time. I looked up and down the street—no police yet. Then I looked at Jacob's building and took a big breath. If somebody was going to rescue Mom and Lucas, it would have to be me.

Three bounds and I was at the bottom of his stairway. I had no idea what I'd do when I got to the top, but I figured I'd think of something. I took another breath and started up.

My tennies didn't make a sound, but it turned out even a little movement made the metal steps grind and clang. I had to creep up to keep them from banging. I knew that as long as he didn't know I was around, Mom and Lucas had a chance. But if he caught me, we'd all be killed.

Jacob's place was five whole stories up, and going slowly

enough to be quiet made it seem like my trip up the stairs was taking forever. With every step I wondered if I'd be in time, if Mom and Lucas were still alive. Would it all turn out okay, or would one of them be dead? I prayed as hard as I've ever prayed in my life that they were okay and that I'd think of some way to make sure they stayed that way.

Every landing was right outside a big set of European windows that opened like doors, just like in our hotel room, but they were all padlocked and the panes were painted over on the inside. When I stepped on the third-floor landing, the stairs let out a huge clang. I held my breath, backed up, and stood absolutely still. Then I looked up to see if Jacob would open his windows and look out to see what had made the noise. Nothing happened, and in a few more seconds I went up again, this time leaning most of my weight on the railing at the bad spot.

When I got to the fourth floor, I could hear a man's voice shouting up above. That was a good sign, I thought, because if Jacob was shouting, that meant there was still somebody alive to be shouting at. But by the time I got to the landing between the fourth and fifth floors, I could hear that the shouting was in Dutch, and there weren't any voices shouting back. That's when I started to shake and I could feel the tears sting in my eyes. I told myself I couldn't cry, I had things to do, even if I didn't know yet what they were. It worked. The tears went away.

Only nine steps left. I thought I'd never get to the

top. I knew I couldn't make a sound this close to Jacob's windows, so I went super slowly, testing every step for the noise it might make before actually stepping on it. Once I made the mistake of looking down and I got so dizzy at the height that I almost lost my balance and had to lean against the wall.

I got to the last step, then very, very slowly I moved my head until I could just see into the room.

There was Mom, tied to a chair. Her back was to me, and there was a dirty gray cloth tied around her mouth and knotted at the back of her head. The room was like an attic with the ceiling sloping down here and there, big and brightly lit, with easels standing all over it.

Jacob was pacing back and forth on one side, yelling into a cell phone and making big, angry gestures with his free hand. His face was so red he looked ready to explode.

Lucas wasn't anywhere.

I pulled my head back. My heart was pounding so hard it felt like it might slam right out of my chest. This was when I should have come up with an idea, but I couldn't think. My mind, which had been working so well, screeched to a sudden stop. I stood there a minute, my eyes closed. It was all I could do to take a breath.

I said to myself, very firmly, "Don't panic," and that stupid little phrase actually helped. At last I could breathe, but I had no idea what to do next. The one thing I'd thought of was to sneak in when Jacob's back was turned and hit him over the head with something, but the windows were tightly closed. Even if I broke one of them and got in, what could I do?

Lucas was gone, but I'd found Mom, and now I couldn't think of any way to save her. I prayed again that God would give me an idea of how to help Mom, and I prayed for Lucas.

I'm not sure how long I stood there, but no idea came. Not one. The nuns weren't around, the police hadn't come, and now God had let me down. I was all alone way up farther than I'd ever wanted to climb, and there was nothing I could do. My eyes filled with tears. I wiped them away and started back down.

Going down was even worse than going up. I had to look at the drop to see where I was going. I made it by leaning on the wall and the railing. My fear of heights added to my terror that something horrible had happened to Lucas already, and something just as bad was about to happen to Mom. I had the feeling there was something simple and logical I should do, but all I could think of was finding another way to get the police to help.

Once down, I went over to the mission. The sign was still there, but I tried the door anyway. Locked. My trip up and down the stairs had seemed to take such a long time, but my watch said it was just 7:10. I looked down the street. There were no pedestrians this far up the Oudezijds Achterburgwal. And this wasn't the kind of neighborhood where there were stores or restaurants where I could find somebody. I ran to the other end of the tiny Achterburgwalsteeg to have a look. No luck there—it was just as empty. No drunken men. No girls. Should I take the time to run down into the busier neighborhood? What if something happened to Mom while I was away?

I ran back to the staircase. I decided go up again, kick in the window to Jacob's room, jump inside, grab an easel, and hit Jacob with it.

My foot was on the first stair when I stopped. I remembered how it had felt looking down from the top and I was totally afraid of being that far away from the ground again. Then I started thinking about Mom and Jacob alone in that room, and my fear of heights didn't matter. I was going to go up again even if my feelings about doing it and my panic about Mom were crushing my chest with fear.

And just when I was, like, being squeezed in the middle between two terrors, I heard a footstep on the street behind me.

It's Jacob, I thought. He heard me, and now he's come to get me.

You can only get just so scared before you stop feeling anything anymore, and this was what did it for me. In that split second I went numb. I thought, if Jacob wants to kill me, he can just go ahead and do it. I turned around calmly, my head up, expecting to find a gun in my face.

But instead of Jacob, there stood Sister Anneke and Sister Katje and a tall woman with dyed blond hair and lots of makeup.

"You're back again, little girl," Sister Anneke said. "Where is your friend?"

"I don't know!" I said in a whisper. Then suddenly, out of the blue, I was flooded with relief that they were there. I started to get tears in my eyes again.

"Why are you crying?"

"Because my mother and my best friend have been kidnapped," I said, my voice kind of half sobbing on the words, "and now Mom is upstairs in this building, tied to a chair, and my friend is gone and I don't know where she is, and I'm afraid she might be dead."

I could tell I sounded hysterical and I wasn't surprised that the three women all looked at me funny.

"You don't believe me," I said. "Nobody ever believes you when you're just fourteen."

The woman who was with the nuns stepped closer and put her arms around me. "I know," she said quietly. Her English was slow, but she pronounced it well. "When I was fourteen, I tried to tell people something. Something important. But no one ever believed me. What is your name?"

"Kari."

"I believe you, Kari."

# Rescue, Part 2

If you're dying to know what happened next, don't worry, I'll get back to that part. But first I want to catch you up on what was happening to Mom and Lucas all this time, beginning when I was still in our hotel room reading the *Time* magazine article.

They'd just sat down at their table in the restaurant when the waiter came over and said, "Someone would like to speak to both of you outside."

"Bill?" Mom said, looking at Lucas with her eyebrows raised. Then, to the waiter, "Would you watch our things for a minute?"

"Certainly, madam."

When they stepped outside, no one was there. A big black Mercedes was pulled up right in front of the restaurant's main entrance, parked with one whole side up on the sidewalk, but they do that a lot in Europe, so Mom and Lucas didn't think anything of it.

The restaurant and hotel were on a quiet street, and just then it was deserted. Mom stepped over to look around the corner for whoever had wanted to talk to them, when suddenly Lucas, who was watching her, felt her wrist grabbed from behind, and her arm jerked around behind her and shoved up high. She yelled, partly because it hurt really bad and partly because she'd just had the meep scared out of her.

Mom spun around to see Lucas with one shoulder shoved up high and her mouth still open with pain. Jacob was standing behind and holding on to her.

"Ms. Sundgren," he said, "I find you with your daughter."

Then, with a little jerk on Lucas's arm that turned her sideways enough to look at him, he said, "I studied your face when you and your mother were standing in line to see the *Third Lucretia*. It took me a moment to place you, then I remembered that we had met before under, shall we say, less than pleasant circumstances. Now I learn from my friend Heri that you and some little friend have been spying on one of *my* friends. I believe, between the two of you"—he looked at Mom, then at Lucas—"you know far too much about my situation. I should have run over you in London, when I had the chance."

So it had been him driving the Jaguar after all.

He turned to the Mercedes, opened the driver's door, and shoved Lucas into the front seat toward the passenger side, as if she were a big bag of potatoes. When he turned around he was holding a gun, pointed straight at Mom.

"You try anything, little girl, and I'll shoot your mother now." Then he pulled Mom over to the door and shoved her in.

"I was hoping my . . . business partner would drive, but alas, I must do it alone. So don't try anything or you'll regret it." Still holding the gun, he started the car and pulled out into the street.

Mom, wedged between Lucas and Jacob, took Lucas's hand and gave it a squeeze.

"Where are you taking us?" Mom asked.

"To a place where we can be alone and I can make some decisions."

This gave Mom a little bit of hope. First, he wasn't just going to take them someplace and shoot them right away. Second, there was a good chance he was going to his studio. And third, Jacob thought Lucas was her daughter. He didn't know I existed, and he sure didn't know I'd be looking for them in all the right places. She squeezed Lucas's hand again.

But Mom's good feelings vanished in only a few minutes, because Jacob didn't turn left toward the central part of the city. Instead, they were driving along a road she knew would take them out of town, into the Dutch countryside

252 — SUSAN RUNHOLT

where Jacob might know of a lonely place where he could kill them.

She was gripping Lucas's hand by now, and wondering what the two of them could do to save themselves, or at least what she could do to save Lucas, when Jacob signaled for a left turn. Almost at the same second she saw a sign saying CENTRUM, with an arrow. They were heading back toward the center of town. Mom took a deep breath.

Why had Jacob driven them the long way around? The answer was clear: it was a route where they'd been farther away from pedestrians and buildings and policemen and places where they might escape. It occurred to Mom then that Jacob had been driving on the inside lane all the way along their route so that Lucas couldn't jump out without landing in the middle of traffic.

Then she had her idea.

What was going on with Lucas during this whole drive? Well, if you think she wasn't scared, you're wrong. Even Lucas the Lionheart, Nerves-of-Steel Stickney, was terrified.

At first she thought it couldn't be happening. This was the kind of thing that happened on reruns of *Charlie's Angels*, not to normal, everyday people like Gillian Welles Sundgren and Lucas Stickney. Even Jacob seemed unreal, like one of those evil snakes you see in Disney movies who have the big smiles with all the teeth but you know it's totally phony.

When she got past that stage, she went through a couple minutes when it was like her brain wouldn't let her think about what was happening. Instead, she thought about stupid things. Like, if Jacob was driving a Mercedes now, did that mean he'd rented the Jaguar in London? And who did he think the "little friend" was that Heri had seen her with?

When her mind finally shifted gears and let her focus on what was going on, Lucas got busy trying to come up with a plan. She thought of jumping out of the car, but she was afraid that if she did, Jacob would shoot Mom. Besides, she'd end up right in the middle of traffic.

In one way it was easier for her than it was for Mom because she didn't know her way around Amsterdam, so she never thought they were going anywhere except his studio.

She figured her chance might come when they got out of the car and Jacob was trying to get them upstairs. She remembered how I almost ran right into Jacob while he was unlocking his door, and she thought that, for just a second when he was getting them into the building, he'd have to take his eyes off his prisoners and get his key into the lock.

It was at that moment, she thought, that she and Mom would have their chance.

Her brother, the Brat Child, had been taking karate lessons for years. He was always running around the house going *"Hi-ya!"* and either kicking high into the air or trying to break something with the side of his hand.

Lucas thought the kicking thing would work best. She figured she'd watch Jacob's eyes, and at exactly the right moment, *bam!* the gun would be flying out of his hand and she'd pull Mom around the corner and down the street toward all the tourists and into a bar. Jacob couldn't very well kill them in the middle of a crowd.

By this time they'd gotten into town. They turned a couple of times then Jacob let out a long word starting with the Dutch g sound that she figured was swearing in Dutch.

They'd taken a wrong turn, and now they were driving right past a huge outdoor marketplace. Some of the stalls were still open, and the street they were on was nothing but one big traffic jam full of people and trucks.

Jacob lowered the window and stuck his head out as if to see how far ahead the traffic jam went.

In that moment Mom turned to Lucas and mouthed the words, *GET OUT NOW!*

Lucas shook her head no.

*GO!* Mom mouthed, and as Jacob pulled his head back in, Lucas fumbled with her door, Mom gave her a push, and she shot out into the crowd.

She ran around behind the car, looked at the license number, then dashed into the market area, elbowing her way into the middle of a crowd gathered around one of the stalls.

For a while she listened to hear if there would be a shot. But she figured Jacob wouldn't risk shooting Mom for fear of being caught. At last she edged out of the crowd and saw the Mercedes back up and pull around the corner.

She looked around for a policeman. There wasn't one in sight.

She ran up to a group of people buying french fries at a stall and yelled out, "Does anybody have a mobile phone? It's an emergency!"

The woman who ran the stall stopped what she was doing. "You need to call someone?"

"Yes, the police!" Lucas said.

"You do not need a telephone," the stall owner responded carefully in a heavy accent. "The police station is just there."

Lucas turned and saw a bunch of police cars in front of a building. She took off running.

"Thanks a lot," she yelled over her shoulder.

A minute later she burst through the door into the station.

"I want to report a kidnapping," she gasped, barely able to talk because she'd been running so hard.

The officer behind the desk just looked at her. He was skinny and had thinning hair, small eyes, and a big jaw. His badge said VANDERWEHR.

"Do you speak English?" she said when he didn't respond.

"Everyone in the Netherlands speaks English," he said, making it sound like he was saying that the Dutch were better than everybody else.

"Okay, I said I want to report a kidnapping."

"You do," he said. "And who are you?"

"My name is Lucas Stickney, and the woman I traveled to Amsterdam with has just been kidnapped by a man named Jacob Hannekroot."

"Jacob Hannekroot? The man from the Rijksmuseum who has been in all the newspapers?" He gave her one of those smiles grown-ups have when they don't take kids seriously. "A man like that is not a kidnapper."

"Yes, he *is* a kidnapper!" Lucas answered, getting mad. "I can show you where he took her, and I have the license-plate number of his car. Hurry! He has a gun."

"A gun," Vanderwehr said slowly. "We have very few guns in the Netherlands."

"Well, *he* has one. He was pointing it at Gillian when he was driving us through town."

"You were in a car with him? This is not making any sense, Miss . . ."

"Stickney. Lucas Stickney." She stopped herself from yelling at him and tried to sound reasonable. "I was in the car with him because I was kidnapped along with Gillian. Gillian Welles Sundgren is her name. Jacob . . . I mean, Mr. Hannekroot came while we were in our hotel having dinner. He had us both get in the car, but Gillian told me to get out when we were stuck in traffic by the big market, and he'll probably kill her for letting me go."

"You have your passport?"

"*No!* I told you, I was kidnapped."

"So, Miss Stickney, you come here with no passport and you say the woman you were traveling with told you to get out of the car, leaving her alone with this famous man from the Rijksmuseum you say is a kidnapper. How do you know this Ms. . . . . Sundgren and Mr. Hannekroot are not having a romance?"

The guy didn't know what he was up against.

She leaned forward so her face was close to his, crossing her arms on the counter between them. "Officer Vanderwehr," she began softly. "Have you ever heard of Ibis Petroleum, the company that lost that multibillion-dollar lawsuit last year?"

"Of course. Everyone in the world has heard of that."

"The attorney who won that lawsuit is Allen Stickney. Perhaps you saw him on television. Allen Stickney is my father. He likes lawsuits, and he's *very* good at winning them."

She leaned forward even farther, and her voice was getting louder. "Three minutes ago I came in here and reported a kidnapping. But instead of doing something to save my friend's life, you're wasting time trying to make me feel stupid.

"*I SWEAR TO GOD*," she shouted, slamming her hand down on the counter so hard the whole office shook, "if anything happens to Gillian, my father will take you and the Amsterdam police to court, and *you will PAY!*"

Vanderwehr picked up a microphone, said something in Dutch, and within seconds two officers were coming out of one of the doors behind the front desk, pulling on their coats.

One of them, a young, good-looking man with dark hair and bright blue eyes, said, "You say a woman you know has been kidnapped? Where is she being held?"

"That's better," Lucas muttered, and led the way out the door.

# Rescue, Part 3

When Jacob's car door slammed behind Lucas at the market, Jacob called Mom a bad name and picked up the gun in a way that made her think he was going to hit her with it. Then he put it back down and held it on his lap, probably afraid the people around them might see it.

"I'll make you suffer for that," he said quietly, and he shifted into reverse, checked his mirrors, and started backward. Finally he pulled the car around the corner they had just passed and into the Quarter. A few blocks later he pulled the car onto the curb, grabbed Mom's left wrist, jerked it around her back like he'd done to Lucas, and shoved her arm up high enough that she let out a yell.

"If you try anything, I'll make you very, very sorry," he said, and put pressure on her arm to make sure she slid out of the car after him.

He held on to her like that, walking her down the

street and around the corner into Achterburgwalsteeg, his other arm around her shoulder as if they were lovers going somewhere for a little privacy.

When he had to unlock the building door and again at the top of the stairs when he had to get into his room, he twisted her arm way up again until she gasped in pain.

In his room he turned on the light, bolted the door, and put the chain on, then let go of her and hit her across the face. "That's for letting the girl out of the car."

The blow almost knocked her down. Her instinct was to make as little trouble as possible so he wouldn't hit her again, but she knew the more she could stall him, the better chance she'd have of being rescued. So she hauled up her courage and spoke.

"You know, the *Third Lucretia* is a phenomenal painting," she began, and she was relieved to see the spark of pride in Jacob's eyes. "How long did you work on it?"

"Off and on for almost four years," he said. He was pulling Mom along with him now as he walked around the room, searching the shelves and tabletops for something.

"And how long have you known Marianne Mannefeldt?"

Jacob looked at Mom, as if he wasn't sure how much he should tell her. Then he shrugged. "Six years. I knew her before she was married."

"So you planned the crime together. How exactly did you manage to kill her husband?"

The question didn't have the effect Mom had hoped. Instead of answering, Jacob swore at her and hit her again with his free hand. Then he found a roll of twine, shoved her down into a straight-backed chair, tied her to the chair, and tied her ankles and wrists. Finally he reached for a dirty paint rag, wrapped it around her mouth, and tied it behind her head.

When he finished, he reached in his pocket for his cell phone, and pressed a number.

Mom had never spoken Dutch really well even when she lived in Amsterdam, because everybody in the Netherlands speaks English. And it had been twenty years since she'd used what little she once knew, so she figured she'd forgotten most of it.

But she remembered some words. Plus she speaks German, and German and Dutch are a lot alike. So as Jacob talked, she found she could understand a lot.

He was talking to Marianne—he called her by name a couple times. He started out asking where she'd been between five and seven. Then he told her about capturing Mom and Lucas. He said something about the restaurant, the car, the daughter at the market, and something about the daughter getting the police. Mom thought Marianne must not have liked what he'd done because when he answered her he was yelling and his face got red.

Somewhere during this part of the conversation she thought she heard a noise outside, but the sound was almost drowned out by Jacob's shouting. He kept yelling "you always" and "you never." When she heard "she knows," "kill," and "dead," she knew he was talking about what he was going to do with her.

After a while she thought they'd started talking about ending the whole relationship because twice Jacob said the word "married" in a sarcastic way.

It was right after Jacob said, "Love? What do you mean, love?" that she heard a woman's voice in the hall, then another woman started shouting at the same time. It became clear that two women were coming up the stairs yelling at each other.

As they reached the landing outside Jacob's door, she heard the sounds of a physical fight. Someone fell, there were big bangs against the wall and the door, and the women kept screaming at each other.

Jacob said, "Just a minute," and he put the phone down on the table, walked to the door, and yelled, "Who's there?" in Dutch.

The sounds of the fight just kept on going.

"What's happening out there?" Jacob yelled, but the only answer was more screaming and a big bang against a wall.

Jacob unbolted the door, leaving the chain fastened, and opened it a crack.

Mom heard a window break behind her at the same moment the chain lock snapped and the door burst open.

Jacob was knocked sideways, and a bunch of bodies swarmed into the room. Tony from the hotel was in front holding the huge fireplace log he'd used to break in. He was followed by three women.

Tony dropped the log and went after Jacob, who pushed him backward and turned toward the door. But a tall woman with dyed blond hair hit him hard in the stomach with her elbow. He doubled over and she, Tony, and two older women with gray in their hair and sensible shoes grabbed him from all sides and got him on the floor.

That was when Mom heard my voice behind her where I'd come through the window.

And just then, over all the noise in the room, we heard the *BEEP-beep BEEP-beep* of a European police siren.

# Good-bye Jacob, and Telling Our Stories

The place was totally chaotic. I couldn't believe how strong Jacob was. It took Tony and two of the women to keep him on the ground, and the whole time he was yelling a steady stream of what I was sure were Dutch swear words. Sister Anneke stood on the landing, shouting down to what must have been policemen below.

"Where's Lucas?" I said, struggling with the knots in Mom's gag.

When I finally got it off her, she said, "Lucas was with Jacob and me in the car until—"

At that very moment, I saw Lucas herself, framed in the big window, two policemen behind her.

"Lucas!" I shouted. Sister Anneke, back inside the studio, managed to find a pair of scissors and cut the twine from around Mom's hands and feet while Lucas and the policemen scrambled in, and the policemen took over for the people holding Jacob down. Mom stood up and turned around, and I could see huge swollen red spots and some blood on her face.

"Lucas!"

"Gillian!"

"Kari!" The three of us hugged each other separately at first, then all together.

By this time Tony was talking to the policemen in Dutch. The two nuns came over to look at the bruises on Mom's face. Mom said she was basically okay, thanked them, then turned to the blonde, whose name turned out to be Hanne.

"Thank you so much for helping with all of this," Mom said.

"You are welcome," she said, with a thick accent. "Kari is lucky to have you for a mother."

"I'm lucky to have her," Mom said, and the two of them hugged. Tony had finished talking to the policemen, and Mom thanked him for his part in the rescue.

Jacob was on his feet, his wrists in handcuffs. A radio was squawking, and I heard the sound of more police cars on the street below.

The head policeman thought Mom should go to the hospital, but she said she was just bruised. She said spending a few hours sitting around in a hospital in a foreign country was all she'd need to top off an unbelievably bad evening. The policeman said okay, he'd have a nurse look at her later.

Then he said we all had to go to the station. We went down the stairs from the inside this time. As we passed the second floor, Hanne said, "This is where I live. The apartment should be empty, but I live here with a friend. I do not know how to say it in English." She said something in Dutch.

"They've taken over the empty space. They're squatters," Tony translated.

"We are squatters," Hanne repeated. "So we have a key for the building that someone made for us, and so . . . so . . ."—she was trying to figure out what to say in English—"when we must get in, I open the door."

Three policemen drove Jacob away in a van. The rest of us went in regular police cars to a special station for Quarter business where we all had to tell our stories and sign some papers.

While we sat there, a reporter came in who wanted to ask us questions. Mom, who hadn't even thought about the newspapers, said no, we were going to talk to a particular reporter. Then she called Bill, who called his friend Johanna, who'd just gotten back from Venice. She came down to the station and made us all go over our stories one more time.

Finally, when it was time to go, I went up to Sister Anneke and Sister Katje and said, "Thank you for helping me, and helping save my mom," and I gave each one of them a hug. Then I turned to Hanne. "Thank you, too. Thank you for believing me," I said, and gave her the biggest hug of all. I got tears in my eyes, and I heard her sniff.

She held on to me. "Be thankful for your good life, little girl."

And I was, more than I'd ever been before. I remembered standing with her in the alley, and how she'd told me that nobody believed her when she was fourteen. I thought maybe she was one of the women in the Quarter who'd been abused when they were young, and when she'd tried to tell her mother or somebody that she was being abused, they hadn't believed her.

"I'm sorry . . . about what happened to you when you were a girl," I said.

She gave me another big squeeze, then let me go.

# A Few Minutes of Fame

RIJKSMUSEUM'S *THIRD LUCRETIA* A FAKE

*American Girls Uncover Crime by Museum Insider*

Rijksmuseum officials revealed today that the recently discovered painting known as the *Third Lucretia*, originally attributed to Rembrandt van Rijn, was forged by Jacob Hannekroot, 45, who earlier today was asked to leave his post as the museum's Curator of Dutch Art.

The crime was brought to the attention of museum officials by Kari Sundgren and Lucas Stickney, both 14, of Saint Paul, Minnesota, U.S.A.

In an exclusive interview, the young women identified Hannekroot as the forger and mastermind of a crime which may implicate the widow of a prominent

Dutch industrialist and involve at least three suspicious deaths.

Mr. Hannekroot was arrested last night after kidnapping American journalist Gillian Sundgren, 43, mother of one of the girls. The young women led a daring rescue of the victim from Mr. Hannekroot's private studio in a secluded street in Amsterdam's Quarter.

The abduction was only the latest incident in a tale that took the girls from the United States to London, Paris, and Amsterdam. . . .

That was the way Bill translated the beginning of the story that ran in the Sunday paper. And right there, at the top of the front page, under the headline, was a picture of us standing next to the *Third Lucretia,* which a newspaper photographer had taken in the Rijksmuseum that morning.

For a while we were famous. Monday morning, there was an actual press conference with lots of cameras. We got on European television and on CNN, and our picture was in the *International Herald Tribune.* Both the Minneapolis and Saint Paul papers called and interviewed us. So did a German newspaper and a French newsmagazine.

Okay, I'm going to admit it right here and now. Having the whole world know what we'd done felt *extremely* cool.

We spent a few more days in Amsterdam making all

kinds of statements to the police. Then, finally, it was time to go home.

Believe it or not, two TV stations and some photographers were waiting for us with cameras when we stepped off the plane, and we got our pictures in the Saint Paul and Minneapolis papers again. For a few days everybody made a big fuss over us, then it all kind of died down.

There's an artist called Andy Warhol—he's the guy who painted those big pictures of the Campbell's soup cans—who said everybody gets their fifteen minutes of fame. Well, I think the *Third Lucretia* thing was ours. We've been famous, we're not famous anymore. Big deal.

By the way, if you're wondering if I still got punished the way Mom said I would after she caught us in the Quarter, the answer is yes.

# Epilogue

It's funny how one thing happening leads to so many other things happening. Personally, I think the very best thing that came out of the whole *Third Lucretia* business was Grandma Stickney's new project.

Probably you remember about Grandma Stickney speaking at that big international women's meeting, right? Well, International Women United, the group she was president of, had their annual meeting right there at the demonstration, and Grandma Stickney's term as president was over and they had to elect somebody else. Except for going to the United Nations in September, she was pretty much done with it. So when she got back home she was kind of let down and depressed. I guess that can happen if you're used to being really busy and suddenly you're not busy anymore.

So when she heard about Sister Anneke, Sister Katje, Hanne, and the mission, she got this idea. She got a bunch of people to fork over money to help start a new program at the mission to give loans to women in Amsterdam's Quarter to make new lives for themselves.

Believe it or not, her biggest donation came from Allen the Meep. He gave her some huge amount, like $50,000 or something. Lucas said she had asked her if it wasn't hard to get money from Allen, and Grandma Stickney had said, "Dealing with your father is hardly a challenge, dear. I'm accustomed to going toe-to-toe with presidents and prime ministers. Besides, I'm still his mother."

Anyway, she let Lucas and me name the program, and we decided to name it after Lucretia. We figured if it hadn't been for her, none of our whole adventure would have happened. And also, like Mom had explained, if Lucretia hadn't killed herself, she might have had to become like the women in the Quarter. So we named it the Lucretia Project.

Hanne was the first person to get a loan. She and her roommate used some of the money to make the first rent payments on an apartment in a different part of town. Also, the nuns said they'd hire her to be kind of a secretary for them if she could learn how to use a computer, so the rest of the money went for her to take a course on word processing and using the Internet.

As she goes back and forth between the Twin Cities

and Amsterdam, Lucas's grandma is keeping us up to date on what's happening with Jacob and Marianne. Jacob's already been tried and convicted of forgery. When that happened, they called and interviewed us again for the two local papers.

They can also get Jacob on the kidnapping. Even though we gave all those statements to the police, Lucas, Mom, and I may have to go back to Amsterdam to testify about that.

The police also found out from Willem Mannefeldt's dead body that he was poisoned. (Are we surprised?) Marianne—who, by the way, was caught trying to escape to Argentina—is saying that she was totally innocent, that Jacob must have poisoned her husband by himself. But Jacob is saying it was all Marianne's idea and she slipped the poison into something her husband ate. So it looks like both of them will be locked up for a long time.

Here's one major bummer. Remember the London woman who said she saw somebody push Bert out in front of that bus? Well, she looked at the picture Lucas had drawn of how Jacob looked in London, and she said she was pretty sure, almost sure, more than 90 percent sure, but not absolutely sure it was the same man. So they dropped the case.

Lucas has started to like a guy named Josh Daniels who she met in a coffee shop. I'm starting to like Aden, a guy who lives in my neighborhood who was in American History with me and has his eyebrow pierced in two places. I expected Mom to be totally freaked when I finally told her about the piercings, but she's handling it pretty well.

Lucas and I are both working on projects for a summer art contest at a community art center. Lucas is drawing a self-portrait. I'm doing a set of hands kind of like the ones in the *Lucretia* painting, holding some peach and yellow roses that are lying on a pillow. We'd both like to win a prize, but mostly we just want our works to be chosen and hung so other people can see them.

After what happened to us in Amsterdam, Mom, Lucas, and I all enrolled in a community ed course in self-defense. Mom's never been very athletic, but she used to take karate when she was younger, and she's the best one in the class. She says that's because every time she has to kick or hit or throw somebody, she thinks about Jacob and that makes her mean.

Speaking of Mom, here's another thing that happened because of the *Lucretia* mystery. She sold her article for el biggo buckso to a new magazine just starting up called *Internationale*. She got her name on the cover of the very first issue. My favorite part was the opening paragraph of her article. It went:

This is the story of how two teenagers from Minnesota lived a tale of adventure involving a woman from ancient Rome, a seventeenth-century painter, forgery and murder, abduction and rescue, disguises and deductions, two continents, three museums, four countries, a criminal hideaway, and two nuns from Amsterdam's famous Quarter.

The article was such a hit that the magazine offered her a job. Mom really wants to take it, especially since they said they'd pay her a lot more than what she's been getting. But it would mean even more traveling and she doesn't know what to do with me since I only have so many school vacations. It's like déjà vu all over again. Lucas and I hope she'll take it, because we think it will mean even more traveling for us.

Lucas seems to be getting along a little better with her parents. Her dad actually asked her the other day if she was serious about being a lawyer. When she said yes, he said if she keeps on getting really good grades he thought she could probably get into Harvard Law School, where he went. I think that's another change that happened because of the *Lucretia* adventure. I think it helped him start thinking of Lucas as a real person.

You wouldn't believe Camellia. She still spends more time shopping in department stores and malls than any other living human being. But lately Grandma Stickney has her calling friends to help raise money for the Lucretia Project, and Lucas and I are beginning to wonder if what she needed all along was just a good cause.

The other day when I got to their house, Lucas put her finger to her lips and led me to Camellia's study. The door was open just a crack, and I could see Camellia on the telephone, sitting at her little desk in front of this huge, ugly painting of a bunch of dalmatians that she bought last time she was in Santa Fe.

It was eleven o'clock in the morning, and Camellia must have been up for at least two hours, and she never even gets as far as breakfast without putting on her make-up. But there she was, no makeup, wearing a pair of horn-rimmed glasses and an old pair of gray shorts and a T-shirt she'd probably used sometime for aerobics class.

She was saying in her accent, "And some of them are single mothers, bringin' up their children in that awful place. Your gift could help some woman make a better life for herself and her little babies. D'you think you and Dennis could do two thousand?"

I looked back at Lucas, and she mouthed the words, "She's been doing it all morning." Then she opened her eyes wide, spread her hands, and gave a big shrug, as if to say, *Don't ask me, I don't get it either.*

Before I leave off, I should probably catch you up on Lucretia herself.

It turns out the Minneapolis Institute of Arts, the National Gallery in Washington, and the Rijksmuseum are going to team up for a traveling exhibit with all three of the Lucretia paintings together. They're calling the show

*Portrait of a Forgery.* They're going to have a panel that tells our story, and they got permission from Mom and the Stickneys to include our pictures. Exhibits like these take time to organize, so we won't have it in the Twin Cities for another eighteen months. Maybe then Lucas and I will have another fifteen minutes of fame.

Before we left Amsterdam, the Rijksmuseum gave each of us a copy of the poster they used to advertise the *Third Lucretia* before they knew it was a fake. It has a big reproduction of Jacob's painting at the top, and something about Rembrandt van Rijn underneath. Both of us got our posters framed, and we each have them hanging in our bedrooms.

I have mine on the wall across from my bed. Beside it I have smaller reproductions of the other two *Lucretia*s and the painting Lucas and I made in London. Lucas has the drawings she made in the Rembrandt room.

Sometimes when I look at Lucretia I think about how hard it was for women in the olden days, and how hard it still is for some women in a lot of places all over the world. And sometimes I think about how the *Lucretia* paintings and Gallery Guy's forgery have made life better for a lot of women—not just the women who are helped by the Lucretia Project, but my mom, and Lucas's mom, and even Lucas and me.

But mostly when I look at the picture I think of the mystery and how we solved it. Last week when Lucas was over, we were looking at the poster and talking about what happened in London and Amsterdam, and Lucas said, "I sure hope we have another adventure sometime."

"I think we will. I think another mystery is waiting for us."

"Really? You think that?"

"I do. I feel it inside. And I think it might not be too long until it happens."

"Happening soon! Sweet," Lucas said. Then she added, "Like, tomorrow would be good."

# NOTES TO THE READER

This is a work of fiction. None of the characters in this book are real people or based on real people. *Especially* not Jacob Hannekroot. The Rijksmuseum is an actual place—one of the world's greatest museums, I recommend you go there as fast as you can[1][*]—but as far as I know, they don't even have a staff position called Curator of Dutch Art. I made that up.

Speaking of museums, there really are paintings of Lucretia in the Minneapolis Institute of Arts and the National Gallery in Washington, D.C. *Belshazzar's Feast* actually hangs in room 23 of London's National Gallery, along with a lot of other Rembrandt paintings. The British Museum is full of unbelievably cool stuff. If you live near any of these places or have a chance to visit them, go take a look. You don't even need to pay—all four have free admission.

By the way, most of the other places in these pages actually do exist as well. I hope this book makes you want to go into the world and find them. But if you follow in the footsteps of Kari and Lucas, you'll discover that a few of the places they visit came straight out of my imagination.

Let me know when you figure out which ones are real and which ones aren't, and tell me if you have an adventure along the way!

---

1. [*]As I write this, the Rijksmuseum is closed for remodeling, although many of their masterpieces remain on display. The building will reopen in 2010.

# Acknowledgments

Authors often begin their acknowledgments by saying they had help writing their book. In my case, this is literally true. As the dedication notes, my daughter, Annalisa, played a big role in writing *The Mystery of the Third Lucretia.* She gave the characters names, physical descriptions, and personalities. Her response to art and travel made their way into these pages. And Kari channels the voice of Annalisa when she was fourteen. Where the kids sound cool, it's probably my daughter's doing. Where they don't, it's all my fault. I couldn't have created this book it without her help, and I am enormously grateful.

Second only to her, thanks to the members of the writers' group Crème de la Crime: Carl Brookins, Julie Fasciana, Scott Haartman, Michael Kac, William Kent Krueger (*Kent* to us), Joan Loshek, Jean Paul, Mary Monica Pulver, Tim Springfield, Anne Webb, and past member Betsey Rhame. They are steadfast friends and superb critics, and their contributions made each chapter of the book better, stronger and smarter. Special thanks to Jean for her proofreader's eye.

I am tremendously fortunate to be represented by the delightful Tina Wexler, who is every bit as good a critic as she is as agent. I am equally lucky to be edited by Tracy Gates—a dream to work with—and to benefit from the talents of the whole Viking team. They care about quality, and it shows.

Pete Hautman's sage cousel helped make this book better. Thanks, Pete. And thanks to Lily Crutchfield for much-needed fashion advice.

I owe much to the Crime Writers' Association of Great Britain and whoever had the brilliant idea of creating a special CWA Dagger Award for unpublished writers of crime fiction. The contest's enlightened rules allowed an American book for younger readers to be considered alongside British works written for adults. I am truly grateful to the 2005 Debut Dagger Award panelists, especially Edwin Thomas and Kate Jones who helped move this book into the marketplace.

Finally, love and gratitude to family members Rusty, Patty, Steve, and Robyn, and many friends, for patience, encouragement, and cheerleading.

*Susan Runholt* shares a love of art, travel, and feminism with her teenage heroines, but maybe not their nerves of steel! After college, she traveled extensively in Europe and lived in Amsterdam and Paris, working as a bank clerk and an au pair. She's also been a waitress, a maid, a motel desk clerk, a laundress, a caterer, and eventually the director of programming for South Dakota Public Television. She now lives in Saint Paul, Minnesota, where she is a fund-raising consultant for social service and arts organizations. *The Mystery of the Third Lucretia* was named runner-up for the Debut Dagger Award by the Crime Writers' Association of Great Britain. You can learn more about Susan Runholt at www.susanrunholt.com.